"I had a great time," Holly said, barely able to force her words above a whisper.

She watched Bob lean toward her, then closed her eyes. She felt every muscle in her body dissolve at the touch of his warm mouth on hers. When he pulled away and she opened her eyes, she could hardly breathe. She knew that the kiss had lasted only an instant, yet she was afraid that in the next few minutes, when she would need the strength to get to her front porch, she just wouldn't have it. *I can't believe it,* she thought. **I just can't believe this happened.**

Dear Readers,

We at Silhouette would like to thank all our readers for your many enthusiastic letters. In direct response to your encouragement, we are now publishing *four* FIRST LOVEs every month.

As always FIRST LOVEs are written especially for and about you—your hopes, your dreams, your ambitions.

Please continue to share your suggestions and comments with us; they play an important part in our pleasing you.

I invite you to write to us at the address below:

Nancy Jackson
Senior Editor
Silhouette Books
P.O. Box 769
New York, N.Y. 10019

A NEW BEGINNING
Oneta Ryan

First Love from Silhouette

Published by Silhouette Books New York

America's Publisher of Contemporary Romance

Other First Loves by Oneta Ryan

Sometime My Love
Tomorrow's Wish
A Time for Us

SILHOUETTE BOOKS, a Division of Simon & Schuster, Inc.
1230 Avenue of the Americas, New York, N.Y. 10020

Copyright © 1983 by Oneta Ryan

Distributed by Pocket Books

ISBN: 0-671-53363-0

First Silhouette Books printing September, 1983

10 9 8 7 6 5 4 3 2 1

America's Publisher of Contemporary Romance

Printed in the U.S.A.

For Daddy,
John H. Fleming,
in loving memory

A NEW
BEGINNING

1

"I didn't think August was ever going to get here. Did you?" Holly Malone asked. "I mean, the summer has been okay," she said, not waiting for her friend to respond, "but I'm always eager for the first Monday in August to roll around so we can get started in soccer again. You know?"

Sue Chambers nodded, then gave the empty pop can a sweeping kick with the inside of her foot, sending it tumbling down the street ahead of them.

"Keep kicking like that, and Coach Gordon may turn you into a forward," Holly said. She raked her short brown hair away from her face and lifted the feathered strands to catch a whisper of a hot Oklahoma breeze.

9

"No thanks," Sue said. "I've been playing defender for three years, going on four starting today. Why would I want to change?" She kicked the waiting pop can again and puffed out her chest. "Besides, I'm not as aggressive as you forwards are."

"Look who's aggressive." Holly giggled. "You're the one who's been kicking that can ever since we left our street. We're within three blocks of the recreation center, and you're still kicking it! I call that aggressive."

"I call that getting limbered up for the first practice of the season."

The first practice of the season. The thought sent a tingle through Holly. This is going to be the best one yet, she told herself. Images of other soccer practices and other games flashed through her mind as she and Sue walked through the neighborhood toward the recreation center. In her mind's eye, Holly saw a younger Holly Malone. A twelve-year-old starting to play soccer for the first time in the seventh grade. A shy girl who seemed to become someone else when she stepped onto the playing field. She liked that someone else. And now, at fifteen, that someone else seemed to be the real Holly Malone—the one she saw when she looked into her mirror each morning.

Holly Malone. Soccer player. Center forward. She smiled, letting her thoughts complete the daydream. Star center forward on a classic team.

"Why are you grinning?" Sue asked.

Sue's words sent Holly's dreams scattering.

"I was just thinking about how nice it would be to play on a classic team next season instead of having to stay in the recreation team ranks again," Holly said.

Sue raised both eyebrows into the mound of tight red curls that hugged her face. "Get ready. I'm going to dribble the can to you."

Holly gave Sue a quizzical glance.

"If you've got your sights set on going classic next season, you're going to need all the practice you can get," Sue said. "After all, anybody can play in the rec leagues. But I've heard that competition is tough on the classic teams. Personally, I don't think I'd want to have to go through trying out every season to see whether or not I was going to make the team." Sue tapped the can with the inside of her foot again. "Here. Get ready."

"Don't be crazy." Holly sighed. "Making the classic league is only a dream. Besides," she said smiling, "I think you're too attached to that old can ever to part with it."

"You may be right," Sue said, dribbling the can along the curb. She tapped it into place with her left foot and then propelled it into the air with a swift lunge of the instep of her right foot. "Doesn't hurt to dream, I guess." The can hit the concrete several yards ahead of them and clattered to a stop. "After all. I'm counting on a few of the dreams and plans we've made this summer coming true. Aren't you?"

"Sure," Holly said enthusiastically. "We've talked about it enough. I don't see how we can miss."

A mischievous gleam highlighted Sue's green eyes. "We can't," she said. "Not the way I see it. I mean, we were sort of known in junior high because we played for the Stingers. But I've got a feeling that in high school that won't be enough."

Holly wanted to believe that it would be enough, but she didn't. It wasn't really enough last year playing soccer on the Stingers, she thought. We'd probably have been more famous if we'd played on the school's basketball team or maybe the swim team.

"We'll do whatever it takes," Holly said.

"Absolutely."

"After all, if we're going to become leaders and move away from the masses, we're going to have to do the things leaders do," Holly said.

"I want to move to the front of the crowd," Sue said, walking past the pop can in the street. "You know. Hobnob with the popular crowd. Do the things that the 'biggies' in school do."

The thought of becoming a leader, of being recognized by most of the kids in school, excited Holly, and she sensed Sue's excitement as well. She paused in the street for an instant and pointed her finger at Sue.

"The way I see it, high school is going to be a new beginning for us," Holly said. "No more plain Holly Malone. No more plain Sue Chambers. This is going to be *our* year."

"You got it. No more being nobodies for us. By the time Christmas is over and the second semester begins, we'll be the talk of the sophomore class," Sue said positively. "Yes sir. Goodbye nobody. Hello somebody."

Holly giggled, dissolving the determined pose she'd struck. "Okay. We'll shoot for that. By the time the second semester starts, we'll be right where we want to be. With a new school, and a new resolve to move ahead . . . our new beginning will be as easy as kicking a soccer ball."

The smile on Holly's lips faded as she glanced across the highway at the clump of girls that had gathered for the first soccer practice of the season. As she and Sue waited for the traffic to subside, Holly thought about her other dream. After Christmas I'll know whether or not I've made it, she told herself. I'll know if I'm going to be on a classic team next season.

Holly and Sue darted across the highway and joined the group of girls clustered around Coach Gordon.

The short, stocky man blew the whistle that hung around his neck and raised his hand into the air.

"Okay, girls. Gather 'round. Everybody take a seat for a few minutes, and let's see where we are this season."

Holly sat on a mound of thick green grass and glanced around her. Most of the faces she saw were familiar. The team has held together pretty well, she thought, remembering how clumsy they all had been three years ago when they first started playing together. We've lost a few girls and gained a few, but it looks like we've got the same team we had last year this time, Holly thought.

"Let me take the roll and see who I'm dealing with," Coach Gordon said. He took a white handkerchief from his back pocket and dabbed at the perspiration beads on his forehead.

Holly listened to the names and quietly counted off each one on her fingers. She paused to answer "Here" to her name, then resumed her count.

"And Abby Turner," Coach Gordon said, finishing the roll call.

Abby Turner? We don't have an Abby Turner on our team Holly thought, glancing behind her at the cute blonde, who had answered to the name. Holly wondered where the girl came from and if she was any good at playing soccer. She knew the girl hadn't gone to Parker Junior High last year, and she didn't remember seeing the girl in the neighborhood during the summer.

Maybe she's a year or two ahead of us, Holly told herself. But that couldn't be true either. The recreation teams were divided by age groups. The Stingers now had entered the fifteen-to-sixteen-year-old category. Abby Turner couldn't be more than a year older than Holly.

There were whispers and mumblings among the girls as Coach Gordon paused to change the order of papers attached to his clipboard.

Before Holly had a chance to ask Sue about the new girl, Coach Gordon began to speak.

"We've got fifteen girls this year. That's three less than the maximum of eighteen that we had last year." He made a quick swipe across his face with the handkerchief again. "Many of you were with me last year," he said. He scanned the faces clustered before him and grinned. "As a matter of fact, all of you were with me last year except our one new team member, Abby Turner."

Heads turned as did Holly's as each girl took one more glance at the new girl.

"Abby comes to us from a rec team in Tulsa," Coach Gordon said. "She and her family are new to our community. Didn't you just recently move here?" Coach asked the girl.

Abby Turner nodded. "In June."

"Well, we're happy to have you and your family as residents of Broken Arrow, and we're all glad to have you on the Stingers."

"Wonder if she's any good," Sue whispered, poking Holly in the ribs to get her attention.

"Me too," Holly answered. And I wonder what position she plays, she thought. Holly knew how well her other team members played. She also knew that she played a little better than most of them. She knew that she stood as good a chance as anyone, and a better chance than some, of being appointed team captain for the season. The only one of the fifteen that she didn't know about was Abby Turner, and before the practice was over, she'd know about her as well.

"I'm going to hold the team to fifteen if I can," Coach Gordon announced. "So look around you. You all are the girls who will be our team this season. As I said, we're three short of where we were last season, but I think that's good. Since the rules stipulate that each of you must play at least half of a game, by holding the team to fifteen players, all of you will be able to play more full games than you did last year."

The news was music to Holly's ears. She hadn't been happy with last season's games because there were so many girls on the team. Occasionally she got to play whole games, but certainly not as often as she liked. She remembered how Coach Gordon tried to tell them at the beginning of the game who would be playing and which half they would be playing in. Holly was glad when he stopped doing that after the first few games. She knew herself that she played better if she didn't know that she was only going to get to play half a game. It wasn't that she deliberately played worse than she normally did. She knew she was a conscientious player, and she tried to do her best each time she was on the field. Yet it seemed as though when she knew in advance that she was playing only a half, her performance was never up to the standards she always set for herself.

Coach Gordon flipped several papers over the top of his clipboard, letting them hang limply in the still afternoon air.

It was a typical northeastern Oklahoma summer day, and not a whisper of breeze blew to fan the scorching rays of the hot August sun. Holly squirmed under the assault of heat and wished she had applied a more liberal coating of sunscreen to her arms and shoulders before she left her house.

"When I call your name, tell me what position you're interested in playing," Coach Gordon said, taking a pen from the pocket of his knit shirt. "You may want to select the position you played last season, or you may want to make a change." He pushed the wire-rimmed sunglasses up on his nose. "I think you all know by now, though, that unless you're playing goalie, your positions will blur from time to time with the defense moving in on the attack and the offense being placed on the defensive." He stepped in closer to the cluster of girls. "You'll get to make a position selection today for practice. But after we've had a chance to work together, I'll make the position assignments for the playing season. Fair enough?"

Holly smiled and thought about how everyone was probably thinking it was fair as long as each of them got to play the position she wanted.

"What about a team captain?" a voice from behind Holly asked.

Holly turned to find the owner of the voice but only saw blank stares from her team-mates.

"I'm glad you asked that, Abby," Coach said. "Our team captain will hold that position for the season, and I'm the one who'll make the decision as to which girl will do the job." He smoothed the dangling papers under the clipboard and held them flat against the back of the board. "I'll base my decision on skills, aggressiveness, and attitude, and I'll make my decision by the end of the month. When the season begins in September, we'll have a team captain."

Abby's interest had answered a question that Holly hadn't let herself ask. Abby must be some player, Holly thought. And she must want to be team captain too.

Holly listened as each girl called out the position she wanted to play. Luckily, most of them wanted to play the same position they had played the previous season. That was good, in Holly's opinion. That meant they'd be a stronger team going into the season. They were used to each other's moves and they were used to Coach Gordon's calls and technique. We'll make the play-offs this year for sure, Holly told herself, remembering how they had missed the play-offs last year by only two games. If I get to be team captain, I'll work so hard, we'll just have to make the play-offs. We'll be regional champions. We'll be state champions. She laughed at herself for her crazy dreams. Then she thought about the dreams she and Sue had had about being leaders and trying to get in with the popular crowd this year at school. Those were pretty crazy too. Fifteen must be the age of dreams, she thought.

Holly came back to reality in time to hear Coach Gordon say, "Abby Turner. Position?"

"Goalie," Abby shouted.

"Goalie?" Coach said, making a notation on his clipboard. "I was hoping we'd have a goalie in the bunch. Sandy Martin decided to drop out of soccer this year, and I was wondering which one of you would be taking her place as goalie. I might have just found my answer," he said. He placed the clipboard on the ground beside him and picked up the soccer ball at his feet. "Okay, everybody on the field. Let's see how rusty we've gotten."

Holly stood and shook her shoulders and arms, then kicked her legs ahead of her and to the side to limber up.

"This is it," Sue panted, jogging in place a few times beside Holly.

Holly smiled at her. This was it. The beginning of the season that could carry her into the classic league. All she had to do was her best. Her best at every practice and every game.

The practice went well, and Coach Gordon seemed to be pleased with the team's performance after the hour-long session.

"I think we're off to a good start," he said, as he motioned the girls into a huddle. He pushed his sunglasses further up his nose and pulled the knit shirt that was damp with perspiration away from his back. "Tomorrow we'll start an hour later. Four o'clock. We'll play from four to five this week and see how that works out. It's still pretty hot at that hour, and we may need to go to evening practices. Let's take it a week at a time and see," he said thoughtfully.

Holly wiped her cheeks and forehead with the back of her hand. "Tomorrow I'm going to remember to bring my water jug," she said to Sue.

"For sure. I can't believe we forgot all about bringing them today. What a couple of dopes!"

Coach Gordon dismissed the group, and Holly and Sue were the first ones to break away from the huddle.

"Good session," Sue said, walking beside Holly.

"Yeah. I think we're going to have a good team this year." Holly thought about the practice and about how she had tried to put everything she had into it. She had played as well today as she ever had last season. At times she thought she might have played better. I played well, she told herself, but I only scored one goal. I only got the ball past that new girl once. She didn't allow herself to think the girl's name, as if omitting her name would make Abby Turner less of a player than she was.

"Coach seemed to think we did okay too," Sue said. "I hope he lets me play defender again this season. I just don't want to change positions. I think I'm pretty good right where I am."

Holly nodded, hoping that Sue would know that she was agreeing and saying, "I hope I get to remain as center forward," both at the same time. She also hoped that she would get selected as team captain, but now after watching Abby Turner play, Holly wondered. She's a good player, Holly told herself.

As Holly and Sue approached the end of the playing field, Holly noticed a tall, slim boy leaning against the hood of an old car. She tried to keep from staring at him but found herself drawn to his sandy blond hair and muscular build.

"Who's that guy in the parking lot?" Holly asked casually.

"I was just going to ask you the same thing," Sue said. "Slow down. Let's take our time, and maybe we can talk to him as we walk by."

"We can't do that! We don't know him."

"That's how you get to know people," Sue said.

Each step took them closer to the end of the field and the parking lot that hugged the side of the playing area.

"What a hunk!" Sue whispered. "What a hunk!"

Holly slowed her pace again and looked casually at the boy, hoping he wouldn't notice her staring. His tanned face and arms added to his athletic appearance. Holly sighed. "He's just about the cutest guy I've ever seen."

"Definitely better than the average," Sue whispered. She giggled and placed her fingertips to her lips as though she was about to tell Holly a secret. "But we're better than average too. We're going to be two of the biggies this year. Remember?"

"You're crazy."

"I know. When we walk by him, you say hello," Sue said. "Just hello. That's all you have to do."

"I can't do that!"

"Then I'll do it."

They were almost in front of the boy when Sue said, "Okay. You do it."

As they strolled past him, Holly looked at

the boy and smiled. She wanted to open her mouth and say "Hello," but the word just wouldn't come. Soccer had helped her to be more outgoing on the field, but deep inside she knew she was still shy Holly Malone. I just can't walk up to a guy and start talking, she thought.

Holly's toes seemed to curl inside her soccer shoes when the blond boy smiled back at her. His deep brown eyes sparkled and added to the smile on his lips.

As Holly and Sue walked past the boy, Sue grabbed Holly's elbow. "You blew it. Why didn't you say something?"

"I tried. But I just couldn't. I knew it wouldn't work."

Holly heard a car door slam behind her and she and Sue both turned toward the noise. The blond boy had started the old car's engine and was slowly backing out of the parking place.

"There he goes," Sue said, as the boy drove past them and out onto the highway.

"Well, I guess that takes care of that," Holly said. "We'll probably never see him again."

"Probably not. But then again, who knows? We might see him at school." Sue raised her eyebrows into her tight red curls that had gotten even curlier from her damp forehead.

"We might see him, and if we do, you can rush up to him and say, 'Aren't you that cute boy I saw at my soccer practice last month?'"

"If I couldn't even squeak out a 'hello,' I probably won't be doing much rushing." Holly chuckled. "We may have to work on our plan some more."

"*You* may have to work on our plan some more," Sue corrected. "I've already got mine set in my mind. I'm ready!"

Holly spent most of the evening thinking about the first soccer practice and about what a good player Abby Turner was. She's going to be a real help to the team, she kept telling herself. And that will be good. Holly knew that they had to play as a team, and not as eleven individuals on a field, if they were to win their games. She wanted to win, and she knew Abby could help them do the job.

"But that's the problem," Holly wrote in her diary. "Abby plays so well that she will probably be selected team captain. And that's something I've wanted for myself for so long."

"Just because you're our only child," she remembered her mother saying, "doesn't mean you can always have everything you want. When you grow up, the world will *give* you very little. You'll have to work for what you get."

"I'll work for it," Holly wrote. "I'll work hard at every practice, and when Coach Gordon has to make a decision on team captain, he'll see that I'm the one for the job."

Holly started a new paragraph and made some notes about the boy she and Sue saw at the soccer field. "He must have been watching us practice," she wrote. "He had an old car that was painted candy-apple red, and it glistened in the sun. I wish I knew who he was. Muscles. You could see his muscles popping out under the sleeves of his T-shirt. I wish I had said hello to him. Why can't I talk to boys? Will I ever be able to talk to boys?" Then she remembered and wrote on the page, "He smiled at me. He had terrific brown eyes."

Holly jotted a note about the plan she and Sue had for school this year, and she wrote, "Sue says she's ready."

Holly knew that she was ready in the sense that she was eager for school to start. She didn't know if she was ready enough to talk to boys she didn't know and be outgoing with people she had never met before, but she would try.

"It's our new beginning," she wrote. "Sue is sure it will work. And I think I am sure, too." Holly paused to gather her thoughts for one final entry at the bottom of the page. She took a deep breath and held the thought in her mind, sighing softly as she began to write.

"I hope my new beginning will include boys."

2

The month of August passed quickly for Holly, and as she stepped into the pleated plaid skirt and slipped into a blue oxford-cloth shirt, she still couldn't quite believe that today was the first day of high school.

She sat on the edge of her bed to gather the school supplies she had stacked on the floor beside the nightstand the night before.

She clamped a handful of notebook paper in the three-ring binder and glanced at last year's school picture of herself, framed and sitting on the table. Holly studied the photograph, then smiled, glad that she no longer looked as young as the girl in the picture. I'm glad I got my hair cut, she thought, staring at the younger Holly's shoulder-length brown hair. The short, feathered hair style she now wore was so much easier to care for, and it was perfect for soccer—off of her neck, with no curls to come undone because of the searing Oklahoma heat and humidity.

She looked at herself in the dresser mirror, then glanced again at last year's picture. The dark brown eyes were the same. Maybe more mascara on her thick black lashes this year. The eyes, Holly thought, staring at herself in the mirror. She took a closer look, opening her eyes wide and then drawing them into a squint. "Not bad eyes," she said to herself, thinking that they were perhaps her best feature. She continued to gaze at her reflection in the mirror, and for an instant she wished that she were a gorgeous beauty who would be envied by all the girls in school and sought after by all the guys. She held the daydream about her and wondered if she and Sue would be able to carry out the plan they had mapped out for themselves. Becoming a leader wasn't going to be easy, she knew that. The popular crowd was not something that one just chose to be in. You have to be born into that set, she had often thought. Sue was determined. Was she right? Maybe you didn't have to be a born leader either. Maybe you just had to be born determined.

She heard the telephone in the living room ring and knew before her mother could call out for her that Sue was calling to let her know she was ready for school.

"Holly. Telephone," her mother said.

Holly rose from the bed and straightened her clothes, then whisked her hair from her face. I'm determined, she told herself. As determined as Sue.

She gathered her notebook in her arms and turned off her bedroom light.

"Coming, Mother," Holly yelled. She thought about the first day of high school ahead of her and whispered, "Coming, world," as she hurried to take Sue's call.

When Holly's mother dropped Holly and Sue off in front of Westview High School, the line of sophomores who had come to pick up their schedule cards was already forming.

"They said to get here thirty minutes early," Sue said, "but it looks as though we should have gotten here about forty-five minutes early."

"No kidding." Holly sighed.

They took their places in line behind the fifty or so sophomores who had arrived ahead of them.

"The line seems to be moving pretty fast," Sue said. She ran her fingers through her tight red curls, forcing them to straighten and promptly recurl in a different position. "Do you see anybody we know?"

Holly looked around her, hoping that she might catch a glimpse of the blond boy who had watched three of their soccer practices during the past month. "I don't see anybody interesting," Holly said, thinking about the boy and his old, shiny red car. *The car. Since he drives his own car, I bet he's a junior or senior,* she thought. *He wouldn't be standing in a line of sophomores.* Holly's spirits lifted at the thought. There was still a chance that she would see him later in the day. *Who knows,* she told herself, *I might even have a class with him.*

They were almost at the head of the line when Sue grabbed Holly's arm.

"Look," she whispered excitedly. "Over there. Marla Baker."

Holly glanced in the direction Sue was pointing.

"That's who we need to be like this year," Sue said. "We need to get into Marla's crowd."

Holly stared at the girl's flowing blond hair and at the way all of her makeup seemed to draw attention to Marla's powder-blue eyes. "Keep on dreaming, Sue," Holly said. She tried to shake the uncomfortable feeling that had begun to settle over her. Marla was beautiful. Even though she was several feet from them, Holly could see that several shades of eye shadow had been applied to Marla's eyes to achieve that "just-right" look that Marla seemed to radiate. Holly thought of how pleased she had been with her own eyes before she'd left the house that morning. She had applied a light coat of mascara and a touch of brown shadow plus a feathering of highlighter on her brow bone. Still, she couldn't help but feel as though she were a "plain Jane" next to Marla.

"Marla's been popular ever since we started junior high," Sue said. "I never wanted to be friends with her then. You know. She just seemed too . . . too . . . something. I don't know what."

Holly nodded. "I know. Marla always seemed to be too something as far as I was concerned, also. She still is."

"Wonder if she's going out for cheerleader again?"

"Probably. Why would she quit? She was football queen last year. A football queen has to go on with it, don't you think?"

Holly and Sue shuffled closer to the head table to pick up their schedule cards. Holly watched as more and more students flocked around Marla Baker.

"She's definitely got what we're after," Sue

said, glancing in Holly's direction. "I think she should be our first target contact."

Holly looked at Marla out of the corner of her eye, then looked at Sue. "You've got to be kidding. She may be what we're after, but we're nothing like her." Holly compared her pleated plaid skirt and oxford-cloth shirt to the clothes Marla wore. The ballet-slipper-style shoes, the colored hose, the preppy-look dress, and the tailored blazer Marla wore flashed the word "expensive" as boldly as a single neon sign blinking off and on in the darkness. Holly sighed and shook her head. "I don't know, Sue. I don't see how we'll ever be in that league."

"I know what you're thinking. But don't you say it. We're going to make it. No more being nobodies. Remember?"

Sue picked up her schedule from the woman at the table, then Holly took hers.

"What'cha got? What'cha got?" Sue asked excitedly.

They stepped behind the table and held their cards side by side before them to compare schedules.

"Only fifth hour," Holly sighed. "We've only got fifth-hour English together and that's all," she said, glancing at the listing of classes on each of the cards one more time just to be sure. "I can't believe it."

"This is awful. We've always been in each other's classes," Sue protested. "How could they do this to us? Don't they know we've got plans?"

Holly stared blankly down the long hallway ahead of them. Traffic in the building was picking up, with the returning juniors and seniors entering the building at a steady pace and more of the sophomores starting to mill around the building searching for that first-hour class.

"I guess we're stuck with it," Holly said. She tried to calm the fluttering in her stomach by telling herself that it didn't matter all that much if Sue wasn't in her classes. "We'll just hang in there and find our own way," Holly said optimistically. "This isn't going to be any different than junior high. Everything will work out."

"Maybe we can find each other at lunch," Sue said. "And we'll be sure and sit together in English."

"For sure."

They started down the hallway, each looking at the room numbers over the classroom doors. Holly smiled casually now and then at students she knew from Parker Junior High, but familiar faces weren't as prevalent as she had expected. She felt as though she were surrounded by strangers, in a strange school, and soon would be isolated from her best friend. What a day this is going to be, she thought, pausing at a doorway that reflected the same number as that of her first-hour listing on her schedule card.

"This is my class," she said. "Guess I'll see you at lunch. Or later."

"Okay. I'll look for you."

Holly watched Sue walk down the hall before she entered the classroom. She glanced at the unfamiliar faces and wished she had seen the blond boy who had been at her soccer practices. There were only a few familiar faces in the crowd. None of them were kids she had known in junior high though. Even Marla Baker had disappeared into the swarm of students.

"Everything will work out," Holly said to herself, then turned and walked into the classroom.

She walked toward a girl sitting at the back of the room and was surprised to see when the girl glanced up at her that it was Abby Turner.

"Abby!" Holly said, as though she had found a long-lost friend. "How are you doing? Gee, I'm glad you're in this class. I didn't think there would be anyone I knew in here."

Abby smiled. "I was sure of it." A strange look crossed her face. "I've never had to begin a school year when I didn't know anybody. If it weren't for the girls on the soccer team, I wouldn't know a soul." She glanced down at her books, then back at Holly. "I thought it wouldn't be a big deal. But it really kind of bothers me. You know?"

Holly nodded, suddenly feeling foolish for thinking her world would fall apart without Sue in her classes. She had never thought of what school would be like if she were in Abby's position. What would it be like to be a stranger in town? She couldn't imagine. She'd lived in Broken Arrow all her life and had gone to school with the same kids for the past nine years. She couldn't imagine how Abby must feel, staring at total strangers.

"Well," Holly said. "You don't have to worry about this class, because I'll help you all I can." The words came as a shock to Holly. She didn't like or dislike Abby really. Abby seemed to be her competitor on the soccer field even though they were on the same team. She knew that if she had any competition at all for the team captain position, it was Abby.

Holly glanced at the smile on Abby's face and felt as though she and Abby suddenly had become kindred spirits. They were two people who knew each other and two people who needed each other's friendship and help.

"What's your schedule?" Holly asked.

Abby hurriedly pulled her schedule card from her books and compared the listing with Holly's.

"I really can't believe this," Holly said, staring at the two identical listings. "I don't believe it! I'm going to know somebody in all of my classes."

"You don't have to sit with me in every class," Abby added, frowning. "I know you have friends you'll want to sit with in some classes. It won't matter, because I'll feel better just knowing that I know you and that I can ask you questions about things I don't understand."

"Don't be crazy," Holly said. "We'll sit together during this class and any or all of the other classes. You just let me know."

The smile returned to Abby's face.

"After all. What are friends for?" Holly asked. "I'll introduce you to the kids I know, and by the end of the day you'll know everybody I know. You won't be the new kid on the block for very long."

"Thanks," Abby said.

Holly and Abby went through their three morning classes as though they were Siamese twins. It felt so natural to be with Abby that Holly almost forgot to look for Sue when she and Abby entered the cafeteria.

"Tell me if you spot Sue," Holly said, as they

wove their way through the crowded cafeteria. Holly placed her tray on an empty table and made room for Abby. "I told Sue I'd look for her and try to have lunch with her."

"I've been looking, but I don't see her. I don't see how you'll ever find her in this crowd," Abby said.

"Me either." Holly opened her carton of milk and continued to glance around the room. "She must go to lunch at a different time. I don't see her."

"I guess it's hard not being in each other's classes, isn't it?" Abby asked.

"It's different. We've just always had classes together."

"I sometimes miss my friends in Tulsa," Abby said. "But Tulsa isn't that far away. Fifteen miles I suppose from my house to my girlfriend's house. We visit. But it still isn't like being in class together, or going to the same school. We don't have the same things to talk about anymore."

Holly wondered if that would happen to her and Sue. Surely not. They always had been able to talk about everything. Being in different classes wouldn't matter.

"I'm glad I got on your soccer team," Abby continued. "During June and July, I didn't know anybody. At least I've made fourteen friends by being on the team."

Holly thought about the team and about the improvement Abby had made. "I'm glad you're on the team too," she said. "You're a much better goalie than Sandy Martin was. This should be a really great year for the Stingers. I think we've all gotten better, and you've been a good addition."

Abby's face took on a crimson glow. "Thanks for the compliment. I don't think I'm all that good, but I do like playing with the Stingers better than the team I played with last year."

"I guess the team and the coach really make a difference. You can love soccer, but if you had a lousy team and a lousy coach, it wouldn't be much fun to play."

Abby picked at the French fries on her plate. "When do you think Coach Gordon is going to select the team captain?"

Holly stiffened in her chair. "He said by September, but September is already here."

"I think you would be an excellent captain," Abby said, pushing the plate of French fries away from her.

"Me too," Holly laughed, trying to shake the tense feeling that had settled over her. She shook her head and hoped that Abby wouldn't take her remark seriously. "I'm only kidding. Really, I think you'd make a good captain."

Holly hated to admit it, but she did think

Abby would be good. She had the skills, the drive, the ability. Abby seemed to possess naturally all the qualities Holly had spent three years trying to develop.

Holly sipped her milk and listened to the cafeteria noises around them. Kids yelled, dishes clanked, and chairs seemed to fight with each other vying for their rightful positions under the table tops.

"Know what I'd really like?" Abby asked, shattering the tension their discussion of team captain had caused.

"What?"

"I'd really like to become good enough to get on one of the classic teams next season. Now don't get me wrong. I know I just said I like the Stingers, and I do. But I'd really like to get on one of the classic teams."

Holly grinned and folded her hands on the table in front of her. "You amaze me. You know it? You just amaze me."

"What are you talking about?"

"I told Sue at the beginning of the season that I intended to work hard and do everything I could so that I could get on a classic team next season." Holly shook her head. "It's no wonder you and I seem to be the only people on the field who are really playing. We're both pushing for the same thing."

"I didn't know you wanted to go classic," Abby said. "What team?"

"Do you mean which team do I want to play on?" Holly asked.

"Yeah. Do you have your sights set on one particular team?"

"No. I just want to get into the classic league. How about you?"

Abby flicked the air with her hand. "I've got it all planned out." She shrugged her shoulders and smiled. "Of course, it probably won't work out that way. But I'd like to become good enough to play on Bob Anderson's mother's team. Hers is one of the best classic teams around. But I guess I don't have to tell you that."

"I wish you didn't have to tell me that," Holly said. "But I'm afraid you're going to have to. I don't know who Bob Anderson's mother is, or what team you're talking about." She frowned slightly. "And who's Bob Anderson?"

"Bob Anderson is the boy who watched us practice a few times this summer. I thought you knew him. His mother, Elaine Anderson, has got the hottest classic team in Tulsa. They just live two doors down from me."

Holly's head reeled. Bob Anderson. He lives two doors down from Abby.

"You know who I'm talking about, don't you?" Abby asked. "He's the boy who drives that old red car." She shrugged her shoulders and took a quick sip of milk. "I tell you, he works on that car all the time. Everytime I go outside, he's lying under that car or leaning under the hood or changing the tires or something. Guys! Who can figure them?"

"I—I know who you're talking about now," Holly said. "I didn't know you knew him. And I sure didn't know that his mother coached a classic team."

"Well, she does. Guess she has for some time. That's why the team she coaches is in Tulsa. When they moved here two years ago, she decided to stay on as coach of the team. So the team lives in Tulsa, and she lives here. Bob plays, too." Abby poked the plastic straw in and out of her milk carton as she talked. "So does his dad. They're all into soccer. I hear his dad is pretty good. Plays on an adult rec team in Tulsa. I think Bob is the only one in the family who plays on a team here."

Holly's new-found knowledge tumbled through her mind like a rolling soccer ball, and she tried to slow the thoughts to put them all in order.

"Sounds like a pretty athletic family," she said. She glanced around the cafeteria at the students who were packed into the spacious room like pretzels in a can. If he lived next door to Abby, why hadn't she seen him here at school yet? "What grade is Bob in?" she asked.

"He's a junior. At Gregory."

"Gregory High? That's across town," Holly said. "Why doesn't he go to school here?"

Abby shrugged her shoulders and pulled a strand of hair behind her ear. "I think he's enrolled in some special technical classes at Gregory. Besides, he has his own car, so I guess he feels that it doesn't matter where he goes to school."

Holly tried to contain the gnawing feeling that hovered in the pit of her stomach. That's the luck I have, she thought. I just find out who he is and in the next minute I find out that he's nowhere around.

"You're lucky." Holly sighed wistfully. "I think it would be super to live two doors away from a guy like him."

"He is pretty cute, I guess," Abby said. "He's nice. I'll say that. Sort of friendly once you get to know him. I've just known him for three months of course, but he's been friendly to me. We kick a few soccer balls around when he's not working on his car."

Holly smiled, hoping the envy she felt didn't show on her face.

"Why don't you come over some afternoon and kick a few balls around with me? We could play on the street and work our way down to his house. If he comes out, I'll introduce you." Abby's blue eyes took on a mischievous glow. "Better yet, the next time he shows up at one of our practices, I'll grab him and introduce you to him then. That'll work just as well."

"Sounds good to me," Holly said, as she and Abby stood up to leave the cafeteria.

3

The first day of school was better than Holly ever imagined it could be. As she sat on the front steps of Westview High waiting for Sue, she thought about all the things she wanted to tell Sue during the walk home.

The thing that's going to surprise her most is how friendly Abby Turner is, Holly thought. When the day started, Holly had just thought it was nice that Abby was in her first-hour class and that she would be in all her classes. "Who would have thought that by now I'd have become friends with her?" she said to herself.

She shifted the stack of books on her lap and wondered why she hadn't noticed Abby's friendliness throughout all their daily soccer practices the past month. Then she remembered how she and Sue had barely noticed Abby on the soccer field. The thought embarrassed Holly now. I guess we thought since we were friends, we didn't need anybody else, she thought. Sue and I weren't willing to give Abby a chance. Not willing until one of us needed her, she reminded herself.

The heat from the marble steps licked at Holly's arms and face. Even though it was the first week of September, the sun was as hot as if it were still August.

I'll be glad when it gets cooler, she thought, fanning her face with her hand. She picked up her books and started up the steps to go back inside the building and look for Sue.

"Don't pay the ransom. I've escaped!" Sue laughed, as she hurried through the doorway.

"Where have you been? I've been dying out here. What took you so long?"

Sue strolled down the steps past Holly and glanced over her shoulder at her. "I got out of gym late. Well, are you coming?" she asked, almost skipping along the sidewalk.

"You're sure in a strange mood. You must have had a better day than you thought you were going to have."

"I did," Sue said. "I had a great day. You know, I think high school is going to be a lot of fun. Oh, it'll be hard. The homework will be, I'm sure. But the fun stuff will be fun."

"Fun stuff usually is fun, silly." Holly walked along the sidewalk beside Sue. "But I think I know what you mean," she added. "I had a pretty good day myself. Did I tell you in English that Abby is in all of my classes? Isn't that incredible?"

"Incredible."

Holly could tell by the distant look in Sue's green eyes that Sue wasn't impressed with her news. The mention of Abby's name seemed to have thrown a chill over their portion of the sidewalk.

"I wondered why you two walked into English class together, and why you were so careful to sit together. I sort of felt lucky that there was an extra desk next to you so I could join you," Sue said. "You and Abby seemed awfully chummy for two people who hardly know each other."

"What do you mean? We know each other. You know her as well as I do." Holly drew her books closer to her chest and took a deep breath. "Abby is new to Westview High. She doesn't have any friends, and she didn't know her way around. She needed someone to show her, and I did it. No big deal."

"Who showed you around? This was our first day."

Holly felt her throat tighten and she tried to keep an open mind about the discussion. "I guess we showed each other around," Holly said. "You know how it is. If you're in a room full of strangers and you see a familiar face, you go to it. It doesn't seem to matter at that point whether or not you like the person. It's just a familiar face."

Sue didn't respond to Holly's remarks, but Holly sensed from the look on Sue's face that she was giving it some thought.

"Besides," Holly added. "I guess you could say that this was my first shot at being a leader. You do remember our plan, don't you? We were going to move away from the masses—"

"The nobodies."

"The nobodies, then, and we were going to move to the front of the crowd. Be two of the biggies. Remember?"

Sue's frown softened. "I remember." She shrugged her shoulders. "I'm sorry for getting all bent out of shape. Guess I was just a little jealous that Abby is in all of your classes and I'm in only one."

"That's okay. I know the feeling. You know, the thought that you might not be in most of my classes really never occurred to me," Holly said. "I thought that because we went through junior high together, high school would probably be the same. I really thought that was going to be the thing that would make our plan work." Holly brushed her short brown hair away from her face and dabbed at the dampness on her upper lip. "I thought it would be easy to get ourselves into the popular crowd because we'd be doing everything together." She glanced down at the sidewalk. "I know you'll make it, Sue, whether I'm in your classes or not. You've got everything mapped out in your head. You know just what you want to do. But I'm not too sure. This deal of showing Abby around today may be the biggest thing I accomplish this semester—as far as our plan goes."

"Wrong!" Sue said emphatically. She grinned and ran her tongue across her eye tooth. "Little do you know that I have great news." She raised and lowered her eyebrows.

"What do you mean?"

"I mean that while you were doing your good Samaritan-Girl Scout act today, I was doing a little mixing and mingling myself."

Holly's eyes widened. "You were?" Her body tingled with excitement. "Tell me more. Tell me more."

Sue paused at the street corner and waited for the traffic to clear, then crossed the street.

"Come on, Sue. You can talk and cross the street at the same time. Get on with it."

"I'm getting. I'm getting." Sue took a deep breath. "My great news is that Marla Baker is in most of my classes," she said. She grabbed Holly's arm and shook it. "And the best part is that we got together in first hour and just sort of stayed together the rest of the day."

"I thought we didn't like Marla Baker," Holly said.

"We didn't like Marla in junior high, but we're going to like her this year. Anybody who was as popular as Marla was in junior high has got to be popular in high school. People are certainly not going to snub last year's football queen," Sue said. "Let's face it. We've stumbled onto the right person at the right time. How can we miss?"

Holly didn't know how, but at the moment things didn't feel as right to her as they obviously did to Sue.

"We haven't stumbled onto anything," Holly said. "I think maybe you have though."

Sue glanced at Holly out of the corner of her eye. "Well, look who's getting crazy now," she said sarcastically. "It was okay for you to pal around all day with Abby Turner, who, I might add, is a nobody and is not going to get us anywhere, but it's not okay for me to become friendly with Marla Baker."

"It's not that way at all," Holly said.

"It looks that way. And I don't understand why."

"You caught me off guard," Holly admitted, uncertain herself why the hairs on the back of her neck seemed to stand on end at the mention of Marla's name. She paused and looked at Sue. "It's just that before we got our schedules this morning, we were both gawking at Marla and talking about her. Now you tell me we're going to become friends with her." Holly shook her head. "I really don't know how that's going to happen. She isn't in any of my classes, and she probably couldn't care less about me. You know?"

"I know," Sue said. "But I think that if I can become friends with her—and and I'm off to a good start—you will automatically be her friend because I am." Sue walked the curb as if it was a tightrope. "I'll admit that Marla isn't wild about me. Not yet. How could she be? We ignored each other for three years in junior high. But we did stick together today. Most of the day." Sue stepped off the curb and added, "Well, I mostly stuck to her and her friends. But it seemed to be okay."

Holly sensed the uncertainty in Sue's voice. "That's good," she said, trying to sound positive for Sue's sake. "Maybe things will work out for you."

"It'll work. I'm sure of it." Sue walked a few more steps, then stopped and held out her hand. "Oh, I forgot to tell you. Did you know that Marla is a sophomore cheerleader? She's on 'A' squad, of course." Sue's feet seemed to glide down the street as she talked of the new subject. "I tell you, Holly, everybody knows her. And she's dating a senior. Can you believe it? Just starting high school and dating a senior? I've even heard he's on the football team here."

"You and I could never do that, but I can see how Marla does it," Holly said. "Marla's been dating for two years already. The biggest thing in our lives was when Randy and Ricky Roselle's mom took the four of us to the movies last year." Holly remembered the brief "romance" she had had with Randy Roselle. They had said they were going together, yet the only place they went was to a movie. Once. With his twin and Sue. And Randy's mother. The rest of the two-week-long romance was spent occasionally walking through the halls in school together. "That was some deal," Holly said, thinking how silly it seemed, looking back on it now.

"Ricky Roselle was okay when I was a kid," Sue said. "Last year. Right now I'm looking for a more mature kind of relationship."

"Like football boys." Holly chuckled.

"Like football boys."

Holly knew exactly what Sue meant. The thought of going with Randy Roselle again made her skin crawl. But football boys? Definitely acceptable. Then the thought of Bob Anderson and his old car floated through her mind. A certain soccer player wouldn't be too bad either, she told herself. Might even be better.

"I just can't help but think everything is going to work out great for us," Sue said, before Holly had a chance to mention Bob Anderson to her. "I also think that being friends with Marla is definitely a step in the right direction. And she does seem to be pretty nice once you get to know her."

"I suppose you're right," Holly said. "We haven't traveled in the same group as Marla, but maybe that's okay. Maybe it will work."

"Of course it will work. And moving out into another group is the backbone of our plan anyway. I tell you, Holly, I think this has been a perfect day. Perfect for you because even though I'm not in most of your classes, you've had Abby to hang around with. And perfect for me because I'm becoming friends with one of the most popular girls in school."

As they walked around the corner and entered their neighborhood, Holly couldn't help wondering what the year ahead held for her. Maybe I want too much, she thought, remembering that she and Sue had decided that they'd be popular by the second semester. She also had made a pact with herself to join a classic soccer team. She thought about the plan and about the notations she'd made in her diary almost every night. Would the new Holly Malone ever be a leader? Would she ever move with the biggies? Would there ever be boys in her life?

"Marla asked me if I was going to join pep club this year. Or the drill team."

Sue's comment snatched Holly out of her daydreams. "Pep club? We can't be in the pep club, can we? We play soccer." Holly turned to Sue, squinting at the afternoon sun that blazed behind her. "What did you tell Marla?"

"I told her that I was."

"You did?" Holly asked. "Sue, you can't join the drill team. How are you ever going to make the practices? We've got soccer practice."

"I know. I'm not going to join the drill team. I'm going to join the pep club, and you can, too, if you want to," Sue said. "I checked it all out. As a matter of fact, that was why I was late a while ago. The pep club sponsor is Mrs. Cannady, the girl's gym teacher."

"I know who Mrs. Cannady is. I take girl's gym, too, you know."

"Do you want to hear this?"

Holly glanced at Sue and nodded. For a brief instant she felt as though she was seeing a different Sue. Someone she had known for only twenty minutes instead of three years. "Spit it out," Holly said, somewhat reluctantly.

Sue's green eyes sparkled with renewed enthusiasm. "Well, it's like this. The pep club meets only one day a month after school. They all sit together in the stands, though, at the football games. We sit in the stands and scream our hearts out, while the cheerleaders stand on the ground in front of us and lead us on to victory."

"Down, girl." Holly didn't know if Marla or Mrs. Cannady had given Sue the pep talk, but she could see by the look on Sue's face and the way that she was talking that joining the pep club was foremost in Sue's mind at the moment.

"So they only have one meeting a month after school. How are you going to make it to the games?" Holly asked. "Soccer. Remember?"

"I told you I've got it all figured out, and I do. The football games don't start until evening. After our soccer practice is over," Sue said. "And the football games are on Thursday and Friday nights. Our soccer games are on Saturday mornings. No conflicts so far? Huh?"

"Okay. No conflicts so far."

"There aren't any, and there won't be any," Sue said. "I joined the pep club today, and I think you should join it, too."

"Sounds fine," Holly said dubiously. She wondered if she wanted to join the pep club or not. She knew she couldn't tell Sue she was uncertain about it. She'd probably hurt her feelings. She wished she had more time to think about it. Suddenly she thought of something. "I'd like to join. But I couldn't join anything like that without talking to my folks about it first."

"I knew you were going to say that. That's why I'm telling you today. So you can get on with it. You can ask your mom and dad tonight, and when they say yes, you can join tomorrow when you go to gym. Mrs. Cannady has the list you can sign lying right on the corner of her desk."

"You make it sound easy," Holly said. "I'll ask them." Maybe by the time I ask them, I'll have decided if it's something I want to do, Holly thought.

"Do ask them. Marla says we have to be in the pep club in order to try out for cheerleader next season."

"I don't want to be a cheerleader. Sue, are we both talking about the same thing? Weren't you just talking about joining the pep club?" Holly asked. "When did you decide that we should be cheerleaders? And where did you get the idea that we could be cheerleaders even if we wanted to?"

"From Marla, of course."

"Of course."

Sue pulled at the soft red curls at her ear. "The way I see it," she said, "football and cheerleading are *the* things to be in at West-view High. I mean, everything else is out. You know?"

Holly opened her mouth to say once more that she didn't want to be a cheerleader, but Sue began talking again before Holly could speak.

"Of course, if we make cheerleader, we'll have to drop out of soccer. Cheerleaders practice all of the time. We just wouldn't have time for soccer."

Holly's head spun. She started to tell Sue that she didn't have any interest in being a cheerleader, but after seeing the starry-eyed look on Sue's face, Holly wondered if Sue would hear anything she might say.

"I'll ask Mom and Dad about the pep club," Holly sighed. But if my dad ever thought I planned to drop soccer for cheerleading, he'd die, she thought. A vision of her dad standing on the sidelines cheering for her floated through Holly's mind and brought a smile to her lips. She knew her dad was proud of her. He went to all her games. He was her biggest fan.

As her house came into view, Holly remembered she hadn't had a chance to tell Sue about Bob Anderson.

"I found out who that cute boy is who's been watching us play soccer."

"Yeah?"

"Yeah. Abby told me. He lives down the street from her. Can you believe it?" Holly's heart fluttered a little, thinking about the plan she and Abby had made. "His name is Bob Anderson. And Abby said she'd introduce me to him sometime."

"Good."

Holly walked beside Sue and waited for her to say more. The boy they had both admired for a month, and all Sue could say about knowing his identity was, "Good." I just can't figure her out today, Holly thought. What's gotten into her?

"I think I might drop out of soccer," Sue said casually. "You know. Marla and her friends are really into cheerleading and football. And after all, football is where the guys are. This year I'm definitely into guys."

"I'm sort of into guys myself," Holly said. "Or at least I'd like to be. But you can't just drop out of soccer. Just like that. You can't do it." Holly's whole world seemed to be turning upside down. One day in high school and she and Sue suddenly were worlds apart. "You said yourself that we could stay in soccer and be in the pep club, too," Holly said. "Let's do both for a while and see what happens."

"I suppose you're right. I was thinking ahead, I guess. I was thinking that if I have to make a choice between cheerleading and soccer, I'm going to go with cheerleading. How about you?"

"It's too soon for me to think about making a choice like that," Holly said. She looked at Sue. "Besides, you know my dad. He would kill me if I decided to drop soccer for cheerleading. I really think you're going to have to handle the cheerleading by yourself."

"Maybe so. I'll handle getting us in with Marla and her friends, and I'll think about moving into cheerleading. And you don't know, maybe after we get into the pep club and your dad goes to a few of our football games, he might not be opposed to you dropping soccer after all, if that's what you decide to do."

"Maybe."

Holly cut across her neighbor's yard and walked toward her house.

"Remember to ask your folks about pep club," Sue called out.

"I will."

Holly stepped onto her front porch and thought about the pep club and about her soccer activities. Lately she had a hard time thinking about soccer without thinking of Bob Anderson, standing on the sidelines of the soccer field. Now she had a name to think about instead of the vague picture of a boy with a red car.

Holly turned the doorknob with a growing

sense of determination and walked into her house. I'll ask Mom and Dad about the pep club, she told herself. Perhaps it was important to belong if she really wanted to be a class leader. At least that was what Sue thought. Why then did she continue to feel a nagging doubt?

4

Holly changed into her shorts and soccer shoes, then ate a sandwich quickly before her mother took her to soccer practice.

"Does Sue need a ride today?" Judy Malone asked. She slipped a pair of honey brown sunglasses over her brown eyes, then put the station wagon into gear and backed out of the driveway.

"I called her," Holly said. "But her line was busy. She didn't mention needing a ride to practice on the way home." She glanced at her mother and decided that if her mother knew all that she and Sue had talked about, she probably would have a fit.

Ever since Holly had walked into the house,

she'd been wondering about how she was going to tell her mom and dad about wanting to join the pep club with Sue. It was going to be a big deal. She could feel it. And she knew it would be an even bigger deal if she didn't ask them at all and told Sue that she did but that they had refused. No, she had to tell them sometime, and she had to decide when. Maybe tonight at dinner. That probably would be a good time, she thought. As good a time as any.

As they approached Sue's house, Judy Malone slowed the car. "Do you want to run in and see if she wants a ride?"

Holly thought for a second, then glanced at her watch. "No, I don't think so," she said. "We're so early today, Sue probably isn't even ready yet."

"Why did you want to leave so early anyway?" her mother asked. "We could have waited ten or fifteen minutes."

"I've been having trouble with my dribbling lately," Holly said. That wasn't the reason, she thought. But how could she say that the tension of the first day of school and her walk home from school with Sue was driving her crazy? She had to get out onto the field early, even if it meant that she'd have to kick the ball around all alone.

"I thought if I got over to the field a little

early, I could get in some practice time by myself."

They pulled into the rec center parking lot, and at the edge of the playing field, her mother brought the car to a stop.

"Looks like you aren't the only girl who wants to get in a little solitary practice," she said, nodding toward the other girl on the field.

The slender blonde moved the ball across the field as deftly as one of the pros on the Tulsa Roughers professional soccer team. Holly knew that only one girl on the team other than herself played that well.

"That's Abby Turner," Holly said. She paused before opening the car door and thought, I wonder if Abby is working off the first-day-of-high-school weirds too?

Abby glanced up and waved Holly onto the field.

"See you later, Mom. Sue and I will walk home."

Judy Malone smiled. "I'll have dinner on the table, so don't be too long."

"I won't," Holly said, thinking that she and Sue could make the walk in fifteen or forty-five minutes, depending upon how much chatting they did.

Holly walked onto the field and left her ball on the sidelines.

"What are you doing here so early?" Abby asked, running toward Holly. She dribbled the ball as she approached.

"Just wanted to get in some extra practice. I could ask you the same thing, you know."

"So ask."

Holly placed her hands on her hips. "Okay. I'm asking. What are you doing here so early?"

Abby kicked the ball with her instep and sent it flying through the air. "I just wanted to get in some extra practice." She laughed.

"Well, while you're practicing, and while I'm practicing, why don't we get into this together," Holly said. "Let me try to get some goals past you." Holly picked up her ball and carried it out onto the field. "If I can get them past you, I can get them past any goalie we're going to play this season. You're the best goalie I've ever seen on a rec team."

Abby's face grew pink, and Holly wondered if it was from the compliment or from the running Abby had been doing before Holly arrived.

The comment surprised Holly almost as much as it apparently had Abby. Holly didn't know whether something inside her had told her the time was right to pay Abby the compliment, or whether the words had rolled out freely because of the friendship they had formed from being with each other all day in school.

"If we keep wasting time talking, Coach Gordon is going to show up and make us work on drills," Abby said. "We'd better get with it."

Holly and Abby managed a few minutes of practice before their other teammates started arriving. When the field had several players on it, Holly motioned Abby off to the side.

"Did you let me get those three goals past you just to make me feel good?" Holly asked, breathing hard and deep.

"No way. I never *let* people score over me. Not even my best friend."

Best friend? Holly knew she had begun to think of Abby as her friend. But best friends? She couldn't be Abby's best friend, because that was what she and Sue were. How can you have more than one best friend?

"I don't know whether or not you let me score those points," Holly said, walking to a grassy area. "But I have to tell you, I'm feeling pretty good about it."

She and Abby sat on a bed of cool, emerald green clover and leaned back on their hands. Holly glanced toward the parking lot.

"Do you think Bob will come by and watch us today?"

"Oh, it's 'Bob' now, is it?" Abby teased.

Holly felt her face flush. "Well, didn't you tell me that was his name? There's no point in calling a guy 'that guy' when you know his name."

Abby laughed. "Don't go into orbit. I was only kidding."

"I know." Holly knew Abby's comment wasn't serious. It was just that these strange feelings of attraction to him were all so new. It was insane to be falling for a guy that you didn't even know. It sure isn't anything like what I had with Randy Roselle, she thought.

Abby picked a three-leaf clover and spun it in her fingertips. "I don't know if Bob will drop by today or not. I didn't see him when I left to come over here today. And that's pretty unusual. He's always outside working on his car."

Holly remained silent for a moment. She took a deep breath and let it out slowly, and with it came some of the feelings she'd been trying to understand. "I think he's just about the cutest guy I've ever seen, Abby."

Abby raised her eyebrows and nodded.

"I think you're just about the luckiest girl in the world, living down the street from him and all." Holly didn't give Abby a chance to speak. "You're lucky. You know?"

"I guess. I never thought too much about it until now," Abby said. "He is cute, I suppose."

Holly tried to laugh. "Oh, great. Now that

I've pointed out what a hunk he is, you will become my competition as well as my friend all in one day."

"Not a chance," Abby said. "He's pretty cute, I admit, but he strikes me as being more your type than mine. Besides, I don't have time to lurk around outside my house and stare at Bob. I've got other things on my mind." Abby stroked the patch of clover with her palm. "I've got my sights on that boy in our first-hour class who sits in front of you. You know. The one with the black wavy hair who's about six feet tall."

Relief flooded through Holly and a smile spread across her face. "I didn't know you liked him," she said. "We'll have to find out who he is and see if we can't get you a little closer to him. Do you want to change seats with me tomorrow?"

"No! I mean, how obvious could we get?" Abby plucked another clover blossom from the patch. "I'll figure out how to get him to notice me without throwing a rope around him and standing on his toes."

"I see your point. But if you need some help, just ask. I'm going to ask you."

Coach Gordon walked onto the field and blew his whistle, the signal for them all to gather around.

"You're going to ask me for what?" Abby asked.

Holly stood, brushed the pieces of grass from her knit shorts, and started to walk toward the center of the field where Coach Gordon was ready to begin. "I'm going to ask you to introduce me to Bob Anderson."

"I was going to anyway," Abby said, smiling.

The practice was a tough one, and Holly wondered if Coach Gordon made it a little tougher on all of them because of Sue. As she stood at the end of the field, breathless from the workout, Holly wondered what could have made Sue twenty minutes late. She knew what a stickler Coach was for being on time for practice. He always said that when one person was late, it affected the whole team, and it certainly had done that today.

Holly and some of the other team members sauntered over to the sidelines. Then Coach Gordon picked up his clipboard and waved the rest to him.

"Hurry up, girls!" he shouted to the stragglers who were still on the field. "I've got a couple of announcements to make before we go."

Holly looked around for Sue. She'd better get going, Holly thought. Coach Gordon is already annoyed with her.

"Okay, girls," Coach said. "I was going to

give you tomorrow off, but I can see from the practice today that we're going to need tomorrow and Thursday if we're going to be ready for the first game on Saturday." He glanced at the clipboard in front of him. "We're going to need to pull together here, and each of you needs to put all you've got into this. I noticed today that we had one or two who seemed to be somewhere else instead of on the playing field." He gripped the clipboard tighter and rested it against his hip. "We don't have room on this team for people who would rather be somewhere else," he said sternly.

Holly knew Coach was right, and she knew that these frank discussions were necessary from time to time, but that didn't make the lecture any easier to take. She thought it was like being lectured by her parents for something she had done wrong. The only thing that made this easier was that Holly knew Coach Gordon wasn't speaking directly to her. She had given it her all today. She did every day. This was one of those "collective" shape-up talks that Coach gave them once in a while. Only this time, Holly wondered if it wasn't a little harsher.

"Now that that's out of the way," Coach said. "I've got one other announcement, then I'll let you go."

Holly watched him flip the papers on the

clipboard and wondered what he could have to say that he hadn't said already.

"I told you at the first practice of the season that I'd have a team captain selected by September."

Holly's heart raced at the words. During the last week of August, her heart had begun to pound every time Coach Gordon opened his mouth, in anticipation of this announcement about team captain. But when they entered September with no announcement, Holly had tried to put the thought out of her mind. But this was it. She knew that the announcement was seconds away, and for an instant she wished she wasn't standing beside Abby.

"This year's team captain has been selected. By me. Based on ability, aggressiveness, attendance at practices, sportsmanship, and knowledge of the game."

Holly felt the electricity building between her and Abby, and she sensed that Abby was as nervous about the announcement as she was. She knew that Abby fit all the categories Coach had mentioned. But then, so do I, Holly thought. So do I.

Without further discussion or hesitation, Coach Gordon said, "The girl I've selected for this season's team captain is Holly Malone."

Holly's heart pounded, and she placed her fingertips over her lips in surprise. She became so light-headed amid the crowd of girls who were all trying to congratulate her at the same time that she thought she might faint.

Abby grabbed her arm. "Congratulations! I knew you would make it."

Holly tried, but she couldn't erase the grin from her face. She had wanted to be team captain for so long. She wondered if she could have congratulated Abby as warmly and as openly as Abby had just congratulated her if the decision had been the other way.

"Look over there," Abby said, pointing to Bob Anderson, who was leaning against the hood of his car in the parking lot.

Holly peered through the group of girls who were walking off in different directions. "How long has he been here?"

"I don't know," Abby said, "but this would be a perfect time for me to introduce you. Just seems natural that Bob might want to meet the captain of our team. Don't you think? I mean, I bet he and his mom know all the other team captains around."

Before Holly could answer, Coach Gordon tapped her on the shoulder.

"I'd like to see you for a minute, Holly, before you leave."

Abby glanced at the coach and then at Holly. "I'll wait for you over by Bob's car."

Holly watched Abby walk away and knew

that now she had no choice. The plan she and Abby had worked out was about to become reality.

Coach Gordon threw his clipboard onto the front seat of his car.

"Congratulations, captain," he said, grinning.

The bark had gone from his voice, and Holly felt a little more at ease as she stood beside him.

"I really appreciate this opportunity," she said shyly. "I'll do a good job, Coach. I won't let you down."

"I know you won't, Holly. If I can count on one girl who consistently plays her best, it's you." He leaned against the car door and folded his arms across his chest. "I selected you as team captain this season because I believe you're the best player on our team," he said. "I think you've played for me long enough to know what I expect from my players and my captains, so I won't go into all of that now. I'll help you as we go along, and I'll expect you, as leader of the team, to help me as well."

"I understand," Holly said soberly.

Coach paused and cocked his head. "Holly, have you ever thought about going classic?"

"Classic! Have I ever thought about it?" She wondered if she should tell him that that was almost all she'd thought about for some time. "I'd love to go classic," she said, trying to keep from sounding too enthusiastic. She didn't want him to think that she didn't want to play on his team anymore, yet she wanted him to know that she had ambition and drive and that she wanted to move ahead with her soccer abilities.

"You're good," Coach Gordon said. "You're good, and this year you're playing better than ever." He smiled at her. "I don't know if that is a conscious effort on your part, or whether you've played so long that it's coming naturally to you, but I've noticed it, and I think that your other teammates probably have noticed it too."

Holly's face felt hot. "I've really been trying," she said.

Coach Gordon rubbed his chin and looked at her thoughtfully. "Let me throw out something here and see what you think about it." He shifted his position against the car. "I think you can make one of the classic teams next season. Probably if you don't do any more than what we do in this season, you'd make it. But I'd like to see you go one better."

Holly wondered what he meant. Every time she walked onto the field, she tried to be better than the time before.

"I'd like to see you work out one-on-one with a private coach for a while this season," Coach Gordon said. "You don't need much help, but I think if you could get a little more individual attention, you'd make classic next season for sure." He paused and rubbed his forehead. "But that's not all I'm thinking about here, Holly. Times are changing. One of the state colleges already offers scholarships to boys in soccer. With the way girls' soccer is growing, I feel sure that in three years, when you start college, girls will be in a position to receive scholarships in soccer as well. As a matter of fact, one of the other coaches told me he knew that would happen within the next two years at Midwestern State."

The thought of going to college on a soccer scholarship excited Holly as much as being on a classic team.

"My parents would love to see me become good enough to win a scholarship," she said enthusiastically. "And I'm ready to shoot for the classics now. When do we begin?"

Coach Gordon chuckled. "We begin as soon as I can find a coach for you." He shrugged his shoulders. "That's the problem. I don't have time in my schedule to work with you. This season I'm having a hard time just coaching the team."

"But if I need help and you can't help me, what are we going to do?"

"I'd like you to talk to your folks about your working with a private coach for a while," he said. "You let me get to work on finding one. How about it?"

"Great! I'll ask Mom and Dad tonight and let you know tomorrow at practice."

"I don't know if I'll be able to find a coach by then, but I'll find one as soon as I can if you think this is something you'd really like to do."

"Are you kidding! I'd love to do it," Holly said.

As she walked away from Coach Gordon, she felt as though she were flying above the ground. This was more than she ever imagined. Team captain. A private coach. Maybe classic next season. Maybe even a college scholarship someday!

She saw Abby waving to her and her heart began to pound harder. She was close enough to see Bob Anderson's face clearly now.

"Holly, I'd like you to meet my friend, Bob Anderson. Bob, Holly," Abby said. "Holly's our new team captain. Just appointed a few minutes ago."

Bob smiled at her, and Holly felt her knees give a little.

"Nice to meet you, Holly."

His half-grin seemed to unlock every muscle in Holly's body.

"Nice meeting you," Holly said, glad that he wasn't one of those people who looked good from a distance but lacked something close up. Face-to-face, he was even cuter than she had imagined. His deep brown eyes captivated her; they were clearly his most striking feature, even compared with his tanned face and sandy blond hair. No, there certainly was nothing lacking in Bob Anderson. Nothing that Holly could see.

Bob's grin broadened. "Your team's pretty good. I've watched you all practice."

"Oh, have you?" Holly asked.

Holly saw Abby roll her eyes and she hoped that Abby wouldn't say or do anything that would give away her nonchalant facade.

"I watch a lot of the teams from time to time," Bob said. "Mostly for my mother. Helps her stay on top of what's going on." Bob folded his arms against his chest. "I can see why you got selected as team captain. I watched you play for a while this afternoon. You're good."

"Thanks," Holly said, flushing. She glanced at the ground and then into his eyes. "I don't think I'm all that good. Not as good as Abby, for sure."

"Hear! Hear!" Abby shouted.

For a brief instant, Holly felt as though she and Bob were the only two people in the world.

"You about ready to go?" Sue said sharply from behind Holly. Sue walked to Holly's side. "I've got to get home."

Holly jumped and blurted, "I've got to get

home, too," before she realized what she was saying.

She saw the puzzled look on Bob's face and watched Abby place her hands on her hips and turn away.

Holly cleared her throat and said, "Before we go, Sue, I'd like you to meet Abby's friend, Bob Anderson. Sue, Bob. Bob, my friend, Sue Chambers."

"Hi," Sue said curtly.

Bob lifted his eyebrows and said, "Hi."

"You ready to go now?" Sue asked.

"I suppose," Holly said.

Holly smiled at Bob. "It was nice meeting you. Maybe I'll see you at practice again sometime."

"Maybe so," he said, smiling back at her. "You never know."

Holly touched Abby's arm as she followed Sue toward the street. "See you tomorrow, Abby."

"Yeah. See ya," Abby said.

As Holly and Sue walked through the neighborhood on the way home, Holly tried to keep from feeling as though Sue had poured a bucket of ice water over her. She walked alongside Sue and didn't make any attempt at conversation. I don't know what's come over her today, Holly thought. She was weird after school and late for practice. She didn't even play that well when she got there.

Holly walked on a little further, until finally her curiosity overwhelmed her.

"Why were you late for practice today?"

Sue stared at her blankly.

"Coach Gordon was really ticked off, or couldn't you tell?"

"I could tell." Sue curled a strand of hair round her finger as she walked. "I was tied up at home and I couldn't get away in time."

"If you needed a ride, you should have called me."

"I didn't need a ride. I was talking to Marla on the phone, and the time just got away from me, that's all. No big deal."

"No big deal?" Holly said. "Coach Gordon nearly ran our legs off and he was harder on all of us because you kept messing up. You think that's no big deal?" Holly shook her head and tried to hold onto her temper. "I really don't understand you today, Sue. You know Coach hates it when any of us is late for practice."

"He'll get over it," Sue said casually. "Besides, what Marla and I were talking about was more important to me than soccer practice."

"What has suddenly gotten to be more important than soccer practice?" Holly asked. "I thought you were as interested in this season as I am. We can't win and make a good showing this season if all of us aren't trying.

When we're at practice, we have to give one hundred percent. Just like at the games."

"Spoken like a true team captain. Rah! Rah!"

A slap in the face couldn't have hurt Holly more.

"Oh, forget that," Sue said, quickly. "I didn't mean anything by that. It's just that I want so much this year, and I'm already trying hard to get everything I want. Don't be mad at me because I was late for practice. Coach was mad enough for the whole team."

"You're right about that." Holly sighed.

Sue tapped Holly on the arm. "Hey, guess what Marla and I were talking about on the phone a while ago."

"What?" Holly said, somewhat reluctantly.

Sue's green eyes took on a mischievous glow. "Marla's going to have a party," she said. She clutched Holly's arm and squeezed it tightly. "And I'm going to be invited. Isn't that terrific!"

"Sure. Sure." Holly tried to understand why Sue would have taken the heat from Coach Gordon just for a phone call from Marla, but then she remembered their resolve to get into the popular crowd. No matter what. *I guess it was important to her,* Holly told herself.

"I tell you, Holly, we're on our way."

"You are on your way."

Sue frowned. "We both are. I'm going to get

an invitation to Marla's party for you too. We planned to be in this together, you know."

"I know," Holly said. "I guess we're really off to a good start. You're going to get us an invitation to Marla's party, and I just got appointed team captain. I guess that's not a bad start," she said, as though she were trying to convince herself.

"Not a bad start at all," Sue said. She walked a few more yards, then said, "Oh, yeah. Congratulations on the team captain thing."

Holly smiled and said "Thanks" as she walked into her front yard. "See you later."

"See ya," Sue said.

5

Holly and her parents had barely sat down to dinner when Holly sprang the news about the special coaching sessions Coach Gordon wanted her to have.

"He said he didn't think it would take very many. Just a few to refine my skills. He said with a little help, I could make classic next season." Holly talked so fast that her parents didn't have a chance to stop her. Her eyes glanced back and forth from her father to her mother as she spoke, watching for a glimpse of acceptance or disapproval on either face. "He even said I might qualify for a soccer scholarship when I'm ready to start college."

Holly looked into her father's eyes. "I'd really like to go for it," she said. "And I don't see any problems with my schoolwork. I made all my classes today. I can handle it," she said confidently, wondering if she really could.

When she paused, her father said, "I think private coaching sessions are a great idea if you want to do it." He looked puzzled, glancing at his wife and then back at Holly. "But I've never heard of girls qualifying for soccer scholarships."

"It's a new deal, Dad," Holly said. "Coach said it is something Midwestern State is working on. It might be available in a couple of years."

Mr. Malone turned to his wife. "What do you think, honey?"

"It's all fine with me," Mrs. Malone said. "I just don't want you to get yourself too bogged down, Holly."

"I won't, Mom."

The thought of being too bogged down with soccer was incomprehensible as far as Holly was concerned. Round one had met with unanimous approval. It was now time for round two, and Holly felt that if she was ever going to get bogged down, it would be now.

She ate most of her dinner and listened while her father elaborated on what a good idea he thought Coach Gordon had in suggesting that Holly get some private instruction. Holly could see that the thoughts of her making the classic league and perhaps someday qualifying for a soccer scholarship excited her father as much as they did her, and she couldn't help feeling proud of her accomplishments on the soccer field.

After her parents' discussion waned, Holly brought up round two: the pep club.

"Sue is going to join the pep club this year, and she asked me if I could, too," Holly said, casually. "They don't have many meetings, and about all they do is sit together at the football games and yell. It really isn't a big thing. But since Sue is joining, I just wondered if you thought it would be all right for me to join, too."

"When are the games?" her father asked. "Won't some of them conflict with your soccer activities?"

"No. The games are on Thursday or Friday nights after the time our soccer practices are over. Sue checked it all out. You know Sue," Holly said. "She wouldn't be in it if it conflicted with soccer." At least a few days ago she wouldn't have been in it if it conflicted with soccer, Holly thought. Who knows about now?

Holly watched her father ponder and wished she hadn't tried to be so convincing. Things would be easier if they would just say no to the pep club, she thought. I haven't really decided yet if I want to be in it or not anyway.

"What do you think, Judy?" Mr. Malone asked.

"Well, I think it will be okay." She turned to Holly and said, "I feel the same way I do about the soccer coaching, though. I just don't want you to get too involved in so many things that you don't have time for your schoolwork. Remember, no one is standing here ready to give you a scholarship for soccer yet. Grades are important. Even if that scholarship does materialize, you'll have to have good grades to back it up."

"I know," Holly said. "Everything will be all right." She took a deep breath. "I'll handle my soccer lessons, and I'll be in the pep club with Sue, and I'll have grades as good as ever. Everything will be all right," Holly said one more time, almost to convince herself. She pulled the pudding dish closer and scooped up a small portion of the chocolate dessert with her spoon. I hope everything will be all right now, she thought, sliding the pudding into her mouth.

Sue accompanied Holly to Mrs. Cannady's office the next day. "I don't know why you didn't do this in gym class," Sue said. "I mean, the roster was lying right there on her desk. It wouldn't have taken a minute to sign up."

"I told you already. The list wasn't on her desk, and I just forgot about asking her when class was over," Holly said. "It still won't take a minute to sign up for pep club anyway. You said so yourself."

They walked into the gym and across the wooden floor to Mrs. Cannady's office. Their feet clacked on the floor and the sound echoed off the concrete block walls, sounding like an army of feet walking through the room.

The door that led to the locker room was open, and the smell of steamy showers and damp towels settled around Holly as she walked past.

"What can I do for you girls?" Mrs. Cannady asked, as she turned the key and removed it from the filing cabinet behind her desk.

"I'd like to sign up for pep club," Holly said. I'd like? she thought. Maybe I should have said that Sue would like me to sign up for pep club.

It didn't matter. She was committed now.

Mrs. Cannady pulled the roster from her desk drawer. "Just sign here," she said, pointing to the next blank line on the sheet.

Holly signed her name and filled in her address as she listened to Mrs. Cannady speak.

"You'll have to purchase one of the pep club T-shirts in the bookstore before Thursday," Mrs. Cannady said. "Our first game is Thursday night, and the pep club will wear jeans and T-shirts. Shoes are any kind you choose, although I imagine most of the girls will be wearing tennis shoes."

Holly placed the pencil on the desk and tried to ignore the uneasy feeling that crept over her.

"That's it," Mrs. Cannady said. "Welcome to the pep club." She smiled at Holly and Sue. "See you girls Thursday night."

Holly and Sue walked out of the gym without speaking. From all the noise their shoes were making, Holly knew that if she spoke, her voice would carry all over the room.

Once outside the gym and in the hallway, she said, "Well, that's that."

There were a few students still in the building as she and Sue walked toward the front door.

"Aren't you excited?" Sue said. "This is going to be the most fun. I just—" She stopped in midsentence and focused all her attention on the well-dressed blonde coming toward them.

"Marla!" Sue shrieked. "What are you doing in the building this late?"

It isn't late, Holly thought. Classes have only been dismissed for about ten minutes.

Marla flicked her long blond hair over her shoulder and shifted her weight to one foot. "I was standing around talking to Lisa about my party, and I'm just now getting out of here. Isn't that crazy? Can you believe we'd stay in here one minute longer than we had to?"

Sue laughed at her comment, but Holly could muster only a forced smile.

"I can't believe you'd do that," Sue said, shaking her head. "That's too much."

Even though Holly was standing beside Sue, she felt as if she were invisible.

Marla laughed. "Anyway," she said, "my party is going to be Thursday night, after the football game. Can you come?"

"Of course I can come," Sue said. "I wouldn't miss it for anything," she added politely.

Holly wondered if Sue was going to mention an invitation for her or if Marla would. I don't really want to go to that party, she thought, glancing from Sue to Marla.

Marla started to walk away from Holly and Sue, but turned back. "Oh, you're invited to my party, too, Holly. Hope you can come," she said carelessly.

"I hope so, too," Holly said. She forced her lips into a smile. "Thanks for asking me." She hoped her words didn't sound as hollow as she felt.

* * *

When Holly's mother dropped her off for soccer practice that evening, Holly could hardly wait to get out of the car and tell Coach Gordon her good news.

"My mom and dad are really pleased about me taking private lessons," Holly said. "Dad was really excited about it. You know how Dad is." Holly moved nervously, shifting her weight from one foot to the other. "Did you find a coach for me?"

Coach Gordon chuckled. "I finally found one." He shook his head and ran his fingers through his hair. "You know I told you I couldn't coach you because I was too busy?"

Holly nodded.

"Well, as it turned out, I found that most of the other coaches in this town are in the same boat I am."

Holly's smile faded. "What does that mean?"

"It means that I was about to give up, but that I struck pay dirt when I called Elaine Anderson." Coach Gordon chuckled to himself again. "It's a good thing. She was just about my last hope."

Holly recognized the name. Elaine Anderson was Bob Anderson's mother. The woman who coached a classic team in Tulsa. The team that Abby wanted to be able to join.

"Is Mrs. Anderson going to be my coach?" Holly asked.

"No. She's snowed under also. But she volunteered her son, Bob. He's played soccer for years, even does some officiating at some of the soccer games in Tulsa."

Holly's eyes widened. Had she really heard him correctly? Did he say that Bob Anderson was going to be her private coach? A lump formed in her throat and she swallowed hard.

"I told Bob to drop by today after our practice, so we could get some kind of schedule worked out for the two of you," Coach Gordon said. "What do you think?"

"I—I think that would be fine," Holly stammered.

"Good. I think your folks will be glad about it too. Anderson's a good player. Knows his stuff. You should be more than ready for the classic leagues after a few sessions with him."

"I'm sure I will be," Holly said, walking onto the field for practice. She remembered how flustered she had become just saying hello to him, and how she'd never been able to talk to boys.

She kicked the soccer ball on the ground before her. If I'd been dating for two years already like Marla has, I wouldn't feel this way, she thought.

* * *

As practice drew to a finish, Holly saw Bob Anderson's shiny red car wheel into the parking lot. She followed Coach Gordon off the field and joined Bob Anderson on the sidelines.

"Holly, Bob," Coach said.

Holly smiled at Bob and at Coach Gordon. "Hi, Bob," she said in a voice that could barely be heard. She turned to Coach Gordon. "We met yesterday. Briefly."

Coach placed his hands on his hips. "Good. Well, if you two have met already, I guess the next order of business is the schedule." He turned to Bob and said, "I guess your mom has filled you in on all of this."

Bob grinned at Coach Gordon. "She filled me in on as much as she knew about it."

"Well, of course I couldn't tell her every detail. That's why I sent for you. You're going to have to help Holly and me work this thing out."

"I'm ready," Bob said.

"Since you're going to be coaching, Bob," Coach continued, "why don't you tell us what days you have available? Then we can see what Holly and I can come up with."

"Tuesday and Thursday evenings are busy for me," Bob said, staring out across the soccer field as though he might find a free night somewhere out there. "I've got soccer practice with my team those nights."

"We practice on Monday and Wednesday afternoons," Coach said. "And all our games are on Saturday mornings."

Holly began to feel like a bug who was off in the air somewhere watching and listening to a conversation of which she was supposed to be a part.

Bob shook his head. "Saturdays are out for me. I do most of my officiating on Saturday mornings and Saturday afternoons."

Coach Gordon rubbed his forehead. "This is getting to be as much of a problem as your mother or I would have had." Coach looked at Holly. "I think you'd be too tired to work out after our practices, don't you?"

"I would be pretty tired, Coach." Today's practice had ended about fifteen minutes earlier, and the muscles in Holly's legs still throbbed.

"I think you're right," Bob said. "I could probably do it after my practices on Tuesdays and Thursdays, but we practice until almost dark. I wouldn't be able to get from there to here and still have time for us to work out before the sun went down."

"What have you got going on Friday evening?" Holly asked.

Bob grinned. "I don't know. What have you got in mind?"

Holly felt her face grow warm, and she hoped she wasn't blushing.

"I'm sorry," Bob said. "I shouldn't have said that. Do you think we might be able to practice on Friday nights?" he added, clearly trying to make amends.

"Friday would be a good night," Coach Gordon said, before Holly could answer.

"Sure," she said. "That's why I mentioned it. I think I could practice on Friday afternoons or early evening."

Coach Gordon clapped his hands together. "Now we're cookin'. Out of seven days, we've got one."

They all laughed.

"I guess we could get some value out of this from one night a week," Coach Gordon said to Holly. "But I'd really like you to work in two practices each week if you could."

"How about Sunday afternoons?" Bob suggested. "Would that be a problem for you, Holly?"

Holly thought for a moment. She and her parents went to church each Sunday morning, but none of them did much of anything on Sunday afternoons. Her dad usually read the Sunday paper and watched whatever sports were on television and her mother read or did needlework. For Holly, during the school year Sunday afternoons meant homework. I can work an hour practice session around my homework, Holly thought, remembering that both her parents had stressed that none of her outside activities was to interfere with her schoolwork.

"I think Sunday afternoons would work for me," she said.

"I can't believe it," Coach Gordon said. "We made it!" He paused for a moment. "We've got Friday evenings—or maybe we should say late afternoon—and Sunday afternoons. Right?"

"Right," Holly and Bob said in unison.

"That's okay with your schedule, Bob?"

Bob pushed his right thumb into the air.

"And you, Holly?"

"Okay by me."

"Guess that settles it then," Coach said. "The practices will be here. And Bob, you just work on the things you feel she needs the most help with. If I pick up anything specific during our team practices, I'll have Holly mention them to you, or I'll talk to her about it and give you a call. Okay?"

Holly and Bob cast inquiring looks at each other and nodded an affirmative to Coach Gordon.

"As I said before, there probably won't be a need for these sessions to go on too long. Four to six weeks is the way I see it now. And of course, Holly, you or your parents can decide to stop at any time." He looked at Bob and grinned. "And if you decide to stop before she does, we'll all have problems."

6

"We are the Rebels. The mighty, mighty Rebels," Holly screamed. Her chant followed the cry of the eight cheerleaders on the ground before her and echoed across the stadium in unison with her fellow pep club members.

When the chant ended, the four boy cheerleaders cupped their hands low in front of them as each of the four girls stepped into the cups and did backward flips, then high scissor jumps.

Marla's golden hair bounced and blew in the crisp night air.

I've got to hand it to her, Holly thought, watching Marla's short, pleated skirt stand out at her sides as her partner led her into another jump and then a spin. She is good.

She's a good cheerleader. I'll have to admit that.

Holly sat beside Sue, and they chanted cheers steadfastly through the first quarter.

"Isn't this great?" Sue said, during one of their short breaks. "Don't you just love this?"

Holly nodded. She glanced around her at all the other girls in her section of the stands. They all wore blue jeans, and they all wore the Westview High pep club T-shirts. Then she caught a glimpse of Abby walking through the stands two sections away from her. Holly had an overwhelming urge to call out to her, but she knew Abby wouldn't be able to hear her above all the noise.

Wonder why she didn't mention that she was coming to the game, Holly thought. Just at that moment, she saw Abby turn and talk to the tall, dark-headed boy behind her. So that's why she didn't tell, Holly said to herself. She recognized the boy as the one who had sat in front of her in first hour. It didn't take Abby too long to get to know him, she thought.

Holly cheered until she thought her voice would leave her completely.

"I wish I could go get a Coke," she muttered to herself.

She remembered that one of the rules that appeared on the two legal-sized pieces of paper she had received today from Mrs. Cannady specifically stated that no one was to leave the stands except at half time. Even then, everyone must be seated again by the time of the kickoff for the second half. Rules. She couldn't believe all the rules. The two long sheets of paper contained nothing but rules. All the things pep club participants can't do, Holly thought. She sat and listened to Sue's strained vocal chords beside her and glanced at Sue out of the corner of her eye. It wouldn't have taken so much paper if they'd just typed up the things we *can* do, Holly thought.

She glanced at Sue again and wondered why her own enthusiasm wasn't building as Sue's seemed to be. I don't like this, she finally admitted to herself. I don't like having to sit here in this group, and I don't like not being able to go get a Coke and go over and talk to Abby. She decided that she probably didn't like what she knew about football much either.

Holly watched Marla flip and twirl and shout and smile. I wonder if I really don't like the pep club and all the rules or if I'm just getting the weirds about going to Marla's party after the game.

It wouldn't be so bad if Abby were going to be there, she thought. She couldn't decide why Abby seemed to be taking a prominent place in her life, but more and more, lately, she found herself wanting to pal around with Abby instead of Sue.

Holly joined in the chants again and tried to put all thoughts of Abby and of Marla's party out of her mind. I have to get into this, she told herself. I'm not being fair to Sue. This is what we wanted, and here I sit being a dope.

"We are the Rebels. The mighty, mighty Rebels," Holly yelled.

When the game ended, Holly followed Sue out of the stands to the ground below. "Where are we supposed to meet your mom?"

"We're not," Sue said. "I changed our plans."

"You mean we aren't going to Marla's party?" Holly heard the lift in her voice and hoped that Sue hadn't noticed.

"Of course we're still going. We're just not going in my mom's car," Sue said. "We're riding over with Marla and Scott. Isn't that great?"

"Who's Scott?"

Sue weaved her way through the crowd toward the stadium gate, with Holly trailing along behind her.

"Scott Lafferty. Number forty-five. I told you Marla was going with him."

Holly thought for a moment. "You told me she was dating a senior."

"Senior. Football player. The whole package."

Holly didn't like the feel of things. She had told her parents that she was riding to Marla's party with Sue's mother. The arrangement was for Sue's mother to take them and for Holly's mother to pick them up. She knew that her parents wouldn't like the idea of her going along in Marla's boyfriend's car. They wouldn't like it at all.

"Marla said they'd meet us here," Sue said, stopping at the main entrance to the stadium. "Wasn't that game just the greatest?"

Holly's thoughts were still focused on what her parents would think about her transportation to the party. "Do you know that my parents would have a fit if they knew that we were riding with Marla and Scott tonight?" she said.

"Yeah. I know. Mine would, too."

"You mean your parents don't know how we're getting to the party?"

"They think I'm riding with you," Sue said casually.

"I don't get it. Sue, how did we get into this?"

Sue looked at Holly and sighed. "Marla asked me if we wanted a ride to the party. She asked me in class today. What was I supposed to say? No, I can't ride with you and your boyfriend—who is a senior and is on the football team—because my mommy is taking me?" She shook her head. "Come on, Holly. Give me a break here. I'm doing everything in my power to make us fit in, and you're complaining about what our parents would think." Sue placed one hand on her hip and shifted her weight to the opposite foot. "They're not going to think anything, because my parents think your mom is taking us and your parents think my mom is taking us. They're happy. And we fit in because we're going to Marla's party with Marla. Everything's okay. Don't worry. I've got it handled."

"I guess you're right," Holly said. "After all, we *are* sophomores now. We aren't babies any more. We should be old enough to do a few things on our own."

"Absolutely."

"I suppose you couldn't very well tell Marla that your mom was taking us," Holly said.

"Not at all. Not after Marla extended a special invitation to us to ride with her." Sue stood on her toes and peered around the crowd of students approaching them. "Here come Marla and Scott now."

Holly searched the crowd for a glimpse of Marla. I guess it's okay, Holly thought, as her gaze rested on Marla and the tall football player at her side. I hope we're doing the right thing.

During the ride to Marla's house there wasn't as much going on in the front seat as Holly had imagined there might be. Oh, sure, Scott had put his arm around Marla and she had kissed him on the cheek a couple of times, but it had been nothing to get upset about.

"I don't know what you expected," Sue whispered to Holly as they stood beside the punch bowl in Marla's dining room.

"I don't know what I expected either," Holly said. "I just figured that someone who's been dating as long as Marla has might do wild and crazy things."

Sue shook her head. "You get me sometimes, Holly. You really get me."

Holly watched Sue move away from the table and decided she might have been wrong to share her thoughts on the car ride with Sue. I've always been able to tell her things before, she thought sadly.

Sue walked toward a group of girls standing in the corner.

I wonder if she's going to try mingling, Holly thought. Not everyone who had been invited to the party had arrived yet.

"Most of the boys will be arriving late,"

Marla had said only minutes before. "Most of them are on the football team, like Scott, and they all wanted to go home and change clothes first."

Holly strolled out of the dining room into the spacious den. Marla's gray stone house was located in one of the new developments in Broken Arrow, and Holly knew the home couldn't be more than one or two years old. In the corner of the den was a bar, and opposite the bar on one of the narrower walls was a massive gray stone fireplace.

More and more people arrived and the large den and dining area began to get crowded. Holly glanced at the faces. Some she recognized from junior high. Most were the kids Marla had run with, people Holly knew only by sight. There were a few strangers in the crowd, and Holly assumed that they were people who were in some of Marla's classes this year but who had attended the other Broken Arrow junior high.

Holly walked into the dining room again to pour herself another glass of punch. Just as she got to the doorway, she heard a commotion coming from the front door. The doorbell rang persistently, and Marla hurried through the den toward the door.

Marla opened the front door and a steady stream of boys filled what little space was left in the den. "The guys have arrived," she shouted.

Holly watched as the girls cheered and the football heroes strutted through the place as if to say, "We have arrived. Let the party begin."

Amazing, Holly thought. Really amazing. So this is what the "biggies'" parties are like. As she stood beside the punch bowl, she tried to decide just what she thought about the whole thing.

Before she could form an opinion one way or another, Sue joined her.

"P. T., huh?" Sue said.

"What?"

"P. T. Pretty terrific, isn't it?"

"The best," Holly said. What else could she say? She knew that was what Sue wanted to hear.

She started to ask Sue about a couple who had moved over to the back corner of the dining room, but before Holly could say anything, Marla walked up to them with a boy on each arm.

"Girls . . . Sue, Holly," Marla said, nodding to each one respectfully, "I'd like you to meet Jeff Peterson and Mike Powell."

"Nice to meet you," Holly said politely.

"Hi, guys," Sue said.

"Jeff and Mike are on the football team. 'A' squad," Marla said. "But I'm sure I don't have to tell you two Rebel fans that. You probably saw every play these two heroes made this evening."

Holly stood there frozen, trying to think of something to say to them.

"Why, of course we did," Sue said easily. "You made our first touchdown tonight," she said, smiling at Mike.

How did she remember something like that, Holly wondered.

"Sue and Holly are on the pep club. They were there in the stand cheering for you," Marla said. "Bet you heard them out there on the field, didn't you?"

Jeff Peterson's blue eyes sparkled. "I heard Holly." He smiled and winked at her. "Heard her all night."

Holly stopped herself from admitting that she had yelled for only half the night. She smiled shyly at Jeff. "Thanks."

Marla released Mike and Jeff's arms and took a step back. "Well, why don't I leave you all and let you get acquainted. I've got to mingle. What kind of hostess would I be if I didn't get around and talk to everybody?"

"She's quite a girl," Jeff said, as Marla walked into the other room.

"She sure is," Sue admitted readily. "And this is really a nice party."

"Yeah," Mike said. "If there's one thing that Marla's good at, it's giving parties."

"What's another thing?" Jeff said sarcastically.

"You probably know better than I do," Mike replied.

Holly began to feel uneasy again. She glanced at Sue and wondered if the smile on Sue's face was genuine or if she was feeling uncomfortable as well.

Jeff rubbed his fingers through his thick black hair and scowled at Mike. "Knock it off, Powell."

Sue quickly stepped between the two broad-shouldered boys. "Mike," she said, smiling up into his brown eyes, "I'd really like to get to know you better, and the traffic to and from this punch bowl makes me feel as though I'm at the Indy 500. Think maybe we might go into the den and talk for a while?"

"Sure, doll," Mike said.

What a move, Holly thought. I couldn't do that. She watched Sue and Mike walk into the den and then it hit her. Now she was alone with Jeff. Their eyes met.

"What a coincidence," Jeff said.

"What?" Holly didn't know what he was talking about.

"I'd like to get to know you better too," Jeff said, smiling. "How about pouring me a glass of that punch and we'll get out of the way too."

Without thinking, Holly poured a glass of punch and handed it to him.

"Thanks."

He gently touched her elbow and guided her across the room. His touch sent a tingle through Holly. She'd never been escorted anywhere by a boy, and even being escorted across a room was a thrill.

Jeff leaned against the dining room wall and took a sip of punch. He smiled at Holly and she grew tense.

"So, Holly," Jeff said, "tell me about yourself."

"What do you want to know?" she asked uncertainly.

Jeff grinned. "Well, let's see. Is this your first year at Westview?"

"Yes." She could feel the tension in her body melting away at the warm tone of Jeff's voice. "How about you? Is this your first year?"

Jeff chuckled. "Sweetheart. You don't make the Rebel 'A' squad as a sophomore. I'm a senior."

Holly's face grew hot, and she was thankful that the lights in the dining room had been dimmed. "Of course," she said quickly. "I knew that. I meant was this your first year on the 'A' squad, and are you a junior or a senior." Her thoughts raced to try to cover her ignorance. "I knew that you had to be a junior or a senior to be on the squad. I bet you made the team last year, didn't you?"

"Sure did. I'm the quarterback," Jeff said. "Guess you knew that from watching me play this evening."

"Absolutely." Holly felt she couldn't very well tell him that football was not her game. She thought it was boring compared with soccer. But she did know enough not to talk soccer to a quarterback on a football team.

As the evening progressed, Holly found it easier to talk to Jeff. Before she knew it, she was laughing and talking with him as if they had known each other for years.

"You're cute, you know it?" Jeff said suddenly.

"Of course," Holly giggled. "That's what all the football guys tell me."

"No, I mean it," Jeff said, stepping a little closer to her.

Holly's heart thundered in her chest. He was standing so close to her that she could smell the heady scent of his cologne.

"How about going out with me next Friday night?"

"I'd love to," she said. The words flowed from her lips so effortlessly and naturally, it wasn't until minutes later that she realized what she had done.

While Jeff talked to her about the movie

they'd go to see, Holly realized that she couldn't just accept a date with a senior. A boy her parents hadn't seen or heard of before. What was she thinking? How could she have done such a crazy thing? She'd never dated before, and here she was accepting a date with someone she'd just met.

At that moment, Holly saw Sue and Mike approaching the punch bowl. "Jeff," she said. "You know Sue, over there, is my best friend. She'd really have her feelings hurt if I made a date at this party and she didn't meet him. Really, Sue was the one who talked me into coming to Marla's party. So, you can see if it hadn't been for her, I wouldn't have met you this evening."

Holly shifted her weight from one foot to the other and wondered how she was doing so far. She couldn't tell by the look on Jeff's face, so she decided to plunge on.

"Do you think it might be all right if we invited Sue and Mike to go out with us next Friday night?" she asked. "I think we'd have a good time. Maybe we could go for pizza instead of a movie." She tried to remember the sultry looks Marla had mastered so well. "I think going out for pizza would be more fun, don't you?" she coaxed. "And if we took Sue and Mike, I'd feel as though I'd paid off my obligation to her."

Jeff frowned at her and shrugged his shoulders. "I don't care," he said. "If you want to invite them, invite them." He sighed and said, "Pizza is okay, too, I guess."

They walked over to Sue and Mike and Sue said, "I guess you know it's about pumpkin time, don't you?"

Holly glanced at her watch. "Good grief. It *is* almost time to go."

"Sad but true," Sue said. "Sad but true."

Where had the evening gone? Holly couldn't believe that a party she'd been dreading so had been such a success.

"It's been nice talking to you, Sue," Mike said.

"Before you two get too wrapped up in your goodbyes, I've got something to ask you," Holly said. She had wondered if her idea was going to work, but now that she saw that Sue and Mike seemed to have hit it off, the big question was going to be a lot easier. "Jeff has asked me out for pizza next Friday night, and we were wondering if you two would like to double with us?"

Holly saw Sue's green eyes light up, and she held her breath in anticipation of Mike's answer.

"I can only speak for myself," he said. "But I think that sounds like a great idea. How do you feel about it, Sue?"

"Are you kidding," Sue said, excitedly. "I'd love it!"

"Good." Holly sighed, relieved to have that matter settled. She turned to Sue. "Now we'd better be going. I'm sure our ride is waiting for us."

Holly told Jeff good night and Sue said good night to Mike. As they headed for the front door, they waved to Marla and shouted their thanks above the heads of the people gathered in the den.

They stepped onto the front porch, and Holly saw her mother's car parked at the end of a row of cars in front of Marla's house.

"Don't say anything in the car about this date," Holly said.

"How can I? I don't know what's going on myself."

"I know. But I'll tell you later. I just don't want my mom to hear us talking about these boys or this date. I have to figure out the right time to tell her."

"Okay," Sue said. "But I still don't see why we have to be so secretive about it."

Holly frowned at her as they approached her mother's station wagon. "Not a word," Holly whispered.

Jeff Peterson's image floated through her mind, and her skin tingled at the thought of such a cute guy asking her out. And he was on the football team. Perfect for our plan, she told herself. She played the evening through her mind once again. I hope I can go out with him next Friday night, she thought. Then suddenly Friday night took on another meaning for her.

Oh, no! Friday night was the night she had soccer practice with Bob.

7

Holly sat on the edge of her bed drying her hair, wondering why her parents had let her go to Marla's party. They wouldn't have done that last year. There was no way that her folks would have let her stay out until one o'clock on a school night. As a matter of fact, she couldn't remember them letting her stay out until one o'clock for any reason.

Things might be changing, she told herself. She brushed the short, feathered strands of brown hair away from her face as the warm air from the dryer swept over her. Maybe things are going to be different now that I'm in high school. Maybe they'll let me go out with Jeff without any hassle after all.

When Holly walked into the kitchen for

breakfast, her dad was already at the table. She walked by the oven to take a peek at the lightly browned rolls inside.

"Good morning, darlin'," Holly's father said, folding a section of the morning paper and placing it on the table beside him. "How was the party last night?"

Holly took her seat to his right and stretched. "It was a lot of fun. It was the getting up this morning that was murder."

"Yeah. I can remember when I was your age," Hugh Malone said, "I could go party with the best of them, but I sure paid for it the next morning."

Holly smiled. "I think I know what you mean," she said, even though she found it hard to imagine her father "partying with the best of them!"

Her mother came in from the utility room and placed a basket of clothes by the kitchen door.

"Have you done a load of laundry already?" Holly asked.

"Only drying," her mother said. "I washed them last night while I was waiting for the time to pick up you and Sue."

Judy Malone went to the oven and removed the freshly baked rolls and placed them on the range top. "How's Mrs. Chambers?" she asked, placing a large roll on each of the three saucers lined up on the counter top.

"Fine," Holly said. She knew she and Sue should have ridden to Marla's party with Mrs. Chambers. She knew her mother would ask. Now they might get caught in their lie, and then that would be the end of the freedom Holly was just beginning to enjoy.

Holly waited breathlessly for her mother to ask her more questions about her ride to Marla's party with Mrs. Chambers, but luckily they didn't come.

As they ate the rolls, Holly watched her mother's expression and then her dad's. This might be a good time to tell them about Jeff, she thought.

She popped the last bite of cinnamon roll into her mouth, then washed it down with a sip of milk. She dabbed at the corners of her mouth with her napkin and folded her hands on the table.

"I met a lot of nice kids last night," she said casually. "Some of them I've never met before."

"Meet any *guys*?" her dad joked.

Holly giggled a little at the way he put such emphasis on "guys." She knew he was making fun of the way she and Sue talked when they were together, but that didn't matter. It didn't bother her to be teased by her parents.

"As a matter of fact I met a very nice *guy*," Holly said. "His name is Jeff Peterson, and

114

he's a senior, and he plays on Westview's football team. He played last night."

Holly thought she saw her father's eyebrows rise slightly when she mentioned that Jeff was a senior.

"Sounds like this Jeff Peterson made quite an impression on you," Hugh Malone said.

"I liked him. We talked for a long time."

"We don't know this boy, do we, Holly?" her mother asked.

Holly shook her head. "No, Mom. He's a senior. I don't remember him at all from Parker when I was there in seventh grade. He must have gone to a different junior high." Holly cast a pleading look in her mother's direction. "He's really nice, though." She lowered her head slightly, almost afraid to look into her parents' eyes. She took a deep breath, then said, "He asked me to go out with him for a pizza next Friday night." Before they could say anything, Holly added, "Sue and this nice guy, Mike, that she met are going too. That is, if you think it would be okay for me to go."

The words were out. Now all she had to do was wait for a verdict.

Holly thought the look in her mother's eyes was favorable. But a troubled look had settled upon her father's face, and Holly felt sure he was going to make her change her plans.

"Isn't Friday night supposed to be reserved

for one of your special soccer sessions?" Hugh Malone asked.

"Yes," Holly said. "But I'll be practicing early, and we won't be going out for pizza until after practice. I wouldn't miss my soccer practice, Dad."

"I know you wouldn't," he said. "I just wanted to be sure that you had remembered it." He placed his cup in its saucer and leaned against the back of his chair. "Well, what do you think, honey?"

Holly glanced at her mother. She had known the question was coming. That was one thing about her parents that she could always count on. They always checked with each other before making a decision where Holly was concerned. Sometimes Holly liked that approach. But there were other times, like now, when she felt the odds might be more in her favor if she didn't have to have a second opinion on everything.

"I don't see a problem," Mrs. Malone said. "I would like to meet the boy before you go out with him, if that's possible," she said to Holly.

Holly smiled and said, "Sure." One opinion was in. She turned to her father for his.

"Does this boy have a car?" he asked.

A car? She stared at him blankly and wondered why it had never crossed her mind to ask Jeff how they would be going to the pizza parlor.

"I—I don't know," Holly said. "I didn't ask him if he had a car. I guess he does. Or maybe he will drive his parents' car."

Her father smiled. "Honey, if that boy didn't spend the evening talking you to death about some old car, then I'll bet he doesn't own one."

Holly felt an "I remember when I was your age" story coming on and hoped that her dad would save the story and give her date a simple okay.

Her mother glanced at her watch and stood up to clear the table. "He probably drives his parents' car, Hugh," she said.

Mr. Malone looked at Holly. "I guess it will be all right with me," he said. "How about you, Jude?"

"It was all right with me five minutes ago," Judy Malone said. She smiled at Holly. "Now get up from there and quit fretting about it. You've got to get to school."

"Thanks, Mom. Thanks, Dad," Holly said. "I'll be ready in a second."

On Friday evening, Holly fixed herself a sandwich and then went into her bedroom to study until it was time to leave for practice. It's all so good, she thought, lying across her bed. My life is wonderful.

When she and her mother drove into the parking lot at the rec center, Bob Anderson was there waiting for her.

"I'm not late, am I?" Holly asked, bounding out of her car.

He shook his head and pulled the soccer ball from the front seat of his old car. "No, you aren't late. I just like to be early when I can. Guess it's a thing with me. I hate to keep people waiting."

Punctual, Holly thought, making one more mental note about him. In her mind's eye she could see the list. Tall. Sandy blond hair. Brown eyes, a deeper shade than her own. Warm, friendly smile. Owns car. Punctual.

Holly waved goodbye to her mother and then turned to Bob. "We might as well get started," she said nervously. "What do you think?"

"I think that's the best idea I've heard all evening," he said. Bob walked onto the playing field ahead of Holly, then paused. He turned to her and asked, "Did Coach Gordon mention anything specific for us to work on today?"

"He didn't say anything to me," Holly said. "Did he call you?"

Bob placed the soccer ball on the ground in front of him and shook his head. "No, I haven't heard from him." He looked at Holly, then glanced out across the field. "Tell you what I think. I think for this first session, we should work on some dribbling techniques." He smiled at her. "I know you're good at this," he said. "I've watched you several times this summer. But I've got a couple of techniques I can show you that I think will improve your speed and your control of the ball."

"You're the teacher," Holly said, shrugging her shoulders.

After about an hour Bob said, "I think that's enough for one day. How about you?"

"I'm with you," Holly said breathlessly. She didn't know what she had expected from these sessions, but she realized that she had thought they were going to be easier than regular soccer practice.

Holly's gaze traveled over the parking lot for a glimpse of her mother.

"Need a ride?" Bob asked.

Holly shook her head. "No. My mom should be here any time. I told her we'd probably practice for an hour or so."

The muscles in her legs throbbed and she reached down and rubbed her calf.

"Sore?"

"Some."

"I didn't mean to wear you out," Bob said. "You should have told me we were going too fast."

"We weren't going too fast. It's just that I'm

not used to being the only player on the field."
She grinned at him. "This is a tough sport."

He smiled back at her. "It is. And you really
play it well."

"You think so? Really?"

"Really," Bob said.

Holly watched him load his gear into his car
and wished her mother would arrive. She
knew she usually wasn't much good at small
talk, although things had worked much better
than she could have ever imagined with Jeff.

When Bob had loaded everything into his
car and slammed the door, Holly felt she
should begin the conversation again. Her
mind raced, trying to think of subjects that
they could talk about without her looking
foolish.

"How long have you been playing soccer?"
Holly asked. There was a subject she knew
something about, and she felt they could probably talk about it indefinitely, or at the very
least until her mother arrived.

"I've been playing since I was in the first
grade." Bob laughed at Holly's startled reac-
tion. "I know. That's a long time."

"It sure is," she said. "You must really love
it. No wonder you're so good. I don't know
anyone who has played soccer that long. I've
only been playing for three years."

"Three years? Is that all? I would have
guessed you were a four- or five-year player at

least. You're really good, you know. I wasn't kidding a while ago."

"I do my best," Holly said, shyly.

Holly wanted to know more about his mother's classic team. Abby seemed to know more about it. At least she knew enough to know that she wanted to be on it.

"Abby tells me that your mom coaches a classic team in Tulsa," Holly said. "Has she been involved with soccer for a long time, too?"

Bob nodded. "For years. She loves it. My dad plays, too. On an adult rec team in Tulsa." He leaned against the hood of his car. "We're all crazy about it," he said. "You know how some people are once they get caught up in soccer. They really get carried away with it, and I guess that's what's happened to our family."

"I know what you mean," Holly said. "I've loved it from the first day I played." She shifted her weight from one foot to another and folded her arms in front of her. "What does your mom look for when she makes her selection of team members?" She glanced down at the ground and then back at Bob. "I guess you know that I really want to join a classic team next season."

"Yeah. Coach mentioned it. Mom looks at skills, of course. And she looks for aggressiveness. That's important to her."

"Aggressiveness," Holly said. "I'm pretty

aggressive I guess, but I probably could be more so. I think I need a little help in that direction."

"It wouldn't hurt any," Bob said. "I made a note to myself on it a while ago. I didn't know if you were holding back out there because of me or if you were just holding back."

"It was probably a little of both," Holly admitted.

"We'll work on it."

Holly noticed her mother pull into the parking lot at the far end of the field. "There's my mom," she said. She started to walk toward the approaching car and then remembered that she didn't know what time they were to practice on Sunday.

"Have you thought about when we should get together on Sunday?"

"It doesn't really matter to me," Bob said. "Three o'clock? Four?"

Holly thought for a second. "Let's go with four o'clock this time."

"Sure. That's fine with me. We can always change it if there's a problem." Bob walked around his car and opened the door. "See you Sunday."

Holly climbed into her mother's car.

"Sorry I'm late," Mrs. Malone said. "Been waiting long?"

"No. Not long," Holly said, glancing at her watch. It was only a little past six. She thought about her date with Jeff. She would still have plenty of time to get ready for it.

Leaning back against the car seat, she allowed her muscles to relax. She thought about Bob. How helpful and friendly he had been! And he was easy to talk to also—really, even easier than Jeff had been. A warm feeling settled over her. And he's a terrific soccer player, she told herself. Did he have a girlfriend? Would he ever ask her out? She tried to force these thoughts from her mind. What difference did it make whether Bob Anderson had a girlfriend or not? Didn't she have a date with the famous Jeff Peterson?

8

The first game of the season was always a tension-filled occasion. Holly walked onto the soccer field and waited near Coach Gordon for her fellow team members to arrive.

Wonder if Bob will be here today, she thought, watching her parents climb into the stands. She hoped he would be. Then he would see for himself if she had learned anything from his coaching.

"You look happy this morning," Coach Gordon said. "How'd practice go last night?"

"Fine, fine," Holly said. "Since you didn't specify what we should work on, we practiced dribbling techniques," Holly said.

"That's okay." Coach looked at Holly and grinned. "Did you learn anything?"

"I think so."

"We'll soon find out, won't we?" Coach said.

"You'll be astounded by my fancy foot-work," she promised.

The Stingers were defeated three to two. Holly had used everything she had, and so had Abby, but their team just couldn't turn themselves around once they started down-hill.

Holly slowly walked off of the field and tried desperately to keep from placing the blame on any one girl. Losing is a part of the game, she told herself. You have to be as good a loser as you are a winner.

Somehow all those sayings didn't have much meaning. Holly knew that their defeat was primarily due to one team player. And that player was Sue.

Sue had been late for the game. And when she was on the field, she seemed to be a million miles away. Holly couldn't remember how many times Sue had let the ball get by her. It was almost as though she deliberately missed making the plays.

As Holly got to the end of the field, she saw Coach Gordon talking to Sue. He had both hands on his hips and a scowl on his face. I hope he's not being too hard on her, Holly thought. And I hope he won't make me say anything to her about how she played or about being late. Maybe he's going to take care of it. A new thought came to her. Some leader I am, she scolded herself. I do okay as long as I don't have to lead. If he puts that responsibility on me right now, I'll crumble into a thousand tiny pieces. I couldn't do that to Sue, Holly thought. Sue's my friend.

"Tough game, wasn't it," a voice said from over Holly's shoulder.

Holly turned to see Abby standing behind her. "Yeah. It was the pits."

Abby grinned. "That's putting it mildly." She nodded toward Sue and Coach Gordon. "What was Sue's problem today?"

"I don't know," Holly said. "I wish I did."

"Well, we gave it our best shot," Abby said. "Can't do much more than that."

"I guess not." Holly watched a few children kick a big red ball across the field and let her disappointment grow. "I just think I should have been able to do something." She ran her fingers through her hair. "As team captain, I should have been able to do something so we would have won that game. We lost only by one point."

"Yes, we lost by only one point," Abby said. "But we all played as well as we could. I'm the goalie. I let that last score get through. You're the team captain, and I'm the goalie. We're not the whole team."

126

"I know," Holly admitted. "But it would have been nice to win this first game."

"It'll be nice when we win the second game," Abby said cheerfully. She looked at Holly. "Hey. How did practice with Bob go last night? I almost forgot about that."

"I'm surprised you remembered."

"Really, I didn't remember," Abby said. "Mom and I just happened to drive by the field last night on our way to the grocery store. I saw you and Bob out here practicing. You were looking good. How'd it go?"

"It went okay," Holly said. "We're going to practice again tomorrow afternoon."

"Must have gone pretty well," Abby said, raising her eyebrows.

"Get hold of yourself, Abby. Our practice schedule is set at Friday evenings and Sunday afternoons. I told you that."

"I know. I just had to tease you a little about it."

"You're one to talk," Holly said. "I saw you at the game the other night with that guy in our first-hour class. I thought it was pretty sneaky of you not to show up for class yesterday too. Looked pretty suspicious, Abby," Holly said. "Pretty suspicious."

"I had a dental appointment," Abby explained. "He pulled a wisdom tooth. See," she said, opening her mouth wide and pointing to the hole.

"Well, how was I to know?" She and Abby laughed together.

Holly's laughter trailed off and she lowered her voice. "While we're on the subject of guys," she whispered. "Do you know if Bob has any girlfriends?"

"Ah-ha! The plot thickens," Abby said.

"Come on, Abby. It was an innocent question."

Abby smiled at her. "You're right. It was an innocent question, and there's my mom," she said, pointing to the car just pulling into the parking lot. "I've got to go."

"Don't I get an answer?"

"Oh, yeah. I didn't know you were in a hurry for it."

Holly shook her head. "If I hadn't wanted an answer, I wouldn't have asked the question, dodo."

Abby grinned. "I don't think Bob has any girlfriends now. There was a girl who hung around at the beginning of summer. I noticed her over there pretty often about the time that we moved in. But I haven't seen her for about a month or more now."

Abby's mother pulled into a parking slot and stopped the car, then honked the horn at her.

"I don't think Bob has time for a girlfriend," Abby said, walking toward the parking lot. "He's too busy playing soccer or working on that dumb car." Abby waved to Holly. "See you later. Have fun tomorrow."

At first Holly was sorry to see Abby leave. She didn't really want to stand there at the end of the field and wait for Sue all by herself. Today, she didn't think she wanted to wait for Sue at all. But she knew she had to.

If I break our pattern, she'll think something's wrong for sure, Holly thought. No, I can't do that. I'll wait and then I'll ask Sue if she needs a ride home. Just like always. Then we can walk to the concession trailer and get a Coke as usual, and then we'll go home.

Holly noticed her parents standing beside the car waiting for her, and she held one finger in the air and pointed to Sue and Coach Gordon.

Just as Holly was about to give up and go home, the discussion between Sue and Coach Gordon broke up. Holly could tell by the expression on Sue's face that she was angry. What could she say to Sue to make her feel better? She didn't want to discuss the game with Sue if she could avoid it.

"Need a ride home?" she asked cheerfully as Sue walked toward her.

"No, I don't need a ride." Sue started to walk past Holly then stopped and looked her square in the eye. "You've sure been standing here a long time. What's the matter? Couldn't you wait to hear the rumors about what happened just now?"

"Sue!" Holly said. "I don't care what you two talked about. I always wait for you after the games. Or you wait for me. Remember?"

"Yeah. Sure. I remember," Sue said. "That was before you became team captain, though. You probably waited for me today for the same reason Coach Gordon wanted to see me. Did he tell you to jump on me, too, for being late and messing up?"

Holly was speechless. "No. Sue, you're wrong." She followed Sue toward the concession trailer. "He didn't tell me to say anything to you."

Holly couldn't imagine why Sue would have been late to the game, especially after being late to practice the other afternoon. She glanced at Sue as they walked and she wondered what on earth had come over Sue. Whatever it is, Holly thought, I'm not going to ask about it. If she wants me to know, she'll have to tell me on her own.

They purchased their Cokes at the concession trailer, then moved to one side to get out of the crowd of people still lined up at its makeshift counter.

"My folks and I are going to the Tulsa Roughers soccer game tonight," Holly said, trying to adopt a light, casual tone. "Would you like to go with us?"

Sue took a sip of Coke and shook her head. "No, thanks," she said sharply. "I've got a date with Mike."

"A date with Mike!" The words leaped out of Holly's mouth before she could stop them. "How did you get your folks to let you go out alone with Mike? My parents hesitated when I asked them about doubling with you next week."

"It wasn't a problem," Sue said. She swirled the cola in her cup. "They think we're going to the Roughers game in Tulsa with a bunch of kids. We're not, though. I just told them that so I wouldn't get a lot of static about going out with him alone."

Holly sipped her Coke in silence. More and more, the girl she had known for so long was becoming a stranger to her. She thought about what her parents would do if they ever found out she had lied to them as Sue planned to do to her parents.

"What are you and Mike going to do tonight?" Holly finally asked. "Or am I not supposed to know?"

"I don't care if you know. We'll probably just ride around in Mike's sports car most of the evening. You know, talk. And get to know each other a little better."

Holly thought for a moment, then asked, "How will you know what to talk about?" She had been wondering about that part of her date with Jeff next week already. It had been fairly easy to talk to him at Marla's party, but she knew she had said just about everything she had to say then. She didn't have any idea what she would talk to him about for a whole evening.

"I'll think up something," Sue said calmly. "It won't really matter what we talk about. We'll be together."

"That sounds a little heavy for a two-day-old relationship."

Sue pulled on a few of the tight red curls at the nape of her neck. "Mike's a fun guy. We've talked on the phone a lot and seen each other a couple of times since the party. There isn't a problem at all. He thinks Marla and I have been friends for years."

"He does? What ever gave him that idea?"

"Not what, Holly. Who," Sue corrected. "I gave him that idea, and that's the idea I want him to keep. If he thinks I've known Marla for a long time, he'll think I've been dating for a long time. And believe me, I'm not about to do anything stupid to make him lose that impression."

Holly looked at Sue but didn't say anything.

"Look," Sue said. "I've always dreamed of dating a football player and being looked up to by everybody. Always. I'm on the verge of getting that, Holly, and I'm not going to let it get away from me."

"I understand," Holly said, even though she didn't really understand.

"If you're smart, you'll do the same thing," Sue said. "You better hang on to Jeff Peterson for dear life, because I've learned from Marla that you're nothing if you aren't dating a football player." She crushed the paper cup in her hand. "I might as well go ahead and tell you what I just told Coach Gordon," she said. "I'm dropping out of soccer."

That was it. The final blow. Holly looked at Sue and waited for the shock to wear off.

"I've decided to devote the next three months to the pep club and to practicing cheers with Marla," Sue said. "We're going to start getting together after school to work out." She threw the paper cup into the trash bin a few feet away. "By the time basketball cheerleading tryouts are held, I'll be ready. You really ought to do that, too," Sue said. "I tell you, Holly. Cheerleading is where it's at."

"I can't do that," Holly said. "I'm taking private lessons with Bob Anderson so I can make one of the classic teams next season. I can't drop out of soccer. I love soccer. I might even get a soccer scholarship to college some day if I work at it."

Sue shrugged her shoulders. "I was just trying to give you a few pointers and help you out," she said. "Don't get trapped into being a nobody all through high school. We did that in junior high. Remember?"

Holly watched Sue walk toward her mother's car in the parking lot. She waved when Sue's mother waved to her.

Before she reached her car, Sue turned once more to Holly. "Take my advice," she said. "Really play up to Jeff on Friday night when we go out. If you don't, you're going to lose him. He may be the only chance you'll get to make a name for yourself this year."

9

You're doing great," Bob shouted from downfield. "Keep going, keep going."

Holly continued to dribble the ball at lightning speed, finally hurtling it toward him with one swift motion of her foot.

"For only three practices, you're really coming along," Bob said.

Holly ran toward him, chasing the ball, then slowed to stop. "Thanks," she said breathlessly. She caught her breath and tried to smile. "Bet you say that to all your students."

"You are all my students." Bob laughed. "And I was being serious. You really do learn fast. Really. If you keep going at this pace, I bet we'll only be with this for four weeks max."

Holly didn't speak and pretended that she was still winded from the workout. Four weeks? They were already into their second week. This was the third practice. How could he tell from the third practice that she wouldn't need more than four weeks of instruction?

"I think you think I'm doing better than I really am," she said, thinking that this couldn't end in four weeks. That would leave only five more practices, she reasoned. Only five more meetings, and I'm just now getting to know him, she thought.

"I guess maybe it is a little too early to make that kind of decision," Bob said. "But I'm really proud of the way you are picking up on the points I've tried to teach you so far."

"As I told you from the beginning, I try hard."

Holly rested her hands on her hips and took several deep breaths then shrugged her shoulders. She instinctively glanced at her watch to check on the time. Usually she watched it to see how many more minutes were left in the hour of practice. But tonight, she watched it for an entirely different reason. Tonight was her date with Jeff, Sue, and Mike. She knew she was going to be on a tight schedule once she left the soccer field, and she knew she couldn't allow herself the luxury of standing around talking to Bob for very long after this evening's practice.

"Do you want to knock off early?" Bob asked.

"No, no," she said. "Why?"

"Well, every time we take a break, you look at your watch," Bob said. "I just thought you might have something you needed to do or someplace you needed to go this evening."

"It's okay. My mom isn't here yet. We can stay with it until she gets here."

Bob glanced at his watch. "It's only about ten minutes until the practice should be over anyway. Why don't we just call it an evening?"

Holly watched Bob load his gear in the car as he usually did. She thought about the evening ahead of her. Jeff Peterson had called her twice and had dropped by the house the night before to meet her father and mother.

I know I'll have a good time, she told herself, watching Bob get everything placed just so in the back seat of his car. But I'm having a good time now, here, talking to Bob.

She leaned against the hood of Bob's car and wished that this strange, confused feeling hadn't settled over her.

"Do you think your mom will be on time this evening?" he asked.

"Oh, yes," Holly said. "I'm sure of it." She wondered why she couldn't bring herself to tell Bob that she had a date.

Bob folded his arms across his chest.

"Why haven't you been watching our team practices much anymore?" Holly asked. Even though she had told herself repeatedly that it didn't matter if he was there or not, she couldn't deny the feeling of disappointment when she didn't see him.

"I've been working on my car a lot," Bob said. He patted the hood gently. "She's got herself a new set of points and plugs now, and clean oil. She's running a lot better, but there are still a few things I have to do to her to get her in really good shape the way I want."

"Oh," Holly said, "you talk about your car as if it were a person. I've never heard anybody call their car a 'her.'"

Bob grinned. "I guess I've spent so much time on her that she's got a personality all her own. I've grown pretty fond of her."

She could see nothing particularly interesting about cars and couldn't really understand why Bob would rather work on his than play soccer or watch her team practice.

He patted the car's shining red top. "I can't speak for everyone, but I guess I'd have to admit I'm attached to this old piece of junk. Best girlfriend I've ever had. She's easy to please."

Holly glimpsed her mother's station wagon enter the parking lot at the far end of the field. Wouldn't you know that her mom would show up the moment the word "girlfriend" entered the conversation!

"There's my mom," she said reluctantly.

"Guess I'll see you Sunday afternoon," Bob said. "Is four o'clock still a good time for you?"

"Sure. Four's fine."

It was exactly an hour from the time Holly walked through her front door to get ready for her date to the time that Sue, Mike, and Jeff rang the doorbell to pick her up. In an hour's time, she had showered, washed and blow-dried her hair, and carefully applied just the slightest bit of makeup to highlight her warm brown eyes and smooth skin.

"Tell them I'll be right there," Holly called to her mother from her bedroom. She slipped on her best pair of jeans and pulled a cream-colored, light-weight sweater over her head, brushing her feathered strands of hair back into their proper places. She glanced at herself one last time in her dresser mirror. "Perfect," she murmured. She took a deep breath and let it out slowly. There's nothing to be nervous about, she thought, wiping her damp palms together. If you run out of things to say, Sue will be there to pick up the conversation.

Everything will be fine, she told herself, then turned out her bedroom light to go meet her guests.

When Holly entered the living room, Sue was sitting on the couch across from Holly's mother. Her father was standing beside the couch talking to Mike and Jeff, who were both standing.

"Hi, everybody. Sorry to keep you waiting," Holly said.

"That's okay," Jeff said. "We were just visiting with your folks."

"Football is one of my dad's favorite topics of discussion." She winked at her dad. "Along with basketball, soccer, boxing, and baseball."

"Are you ready to go?" Sue asked from her seated position on the couch.

"As ready as I'll ever be," Holly said.

Sue stood and was the first one at the front door. "Let's hit it," she said, opening the door.

Holly's father looked at his watch and then at her. "It's seven-thirty now, Holly. I think you should be in by ten. How about it?"

Holly smiled. "Sure, Dad. Ten's fine. See you then." She waved to her mother across the room. "See you later."

When they reached the sleek white sports car parked at the curb, Mike opened the door on the passenger side and Holly and Jeff crawled into the back seat.

Holly moved as far to the other side of the car as she could, allowing Jeff as much space as possible in the small car. She peered over the driver's seat to get a better glimpse of the dash and instrument panel. This is really something, she thought. I can't believe this car is his.

As Mike got in and started the engine, Holly thought about all the kids she knew who owned cars. She didn't know many, and of the ones she did know, none of them had a car as nice as this one. Some of the parents didn't have a car as nice as this.

"You girls got any place special in mind?" Mike asked, pulling the purring machine away from the curb.

The back seat of the car was so cramped that Jeff's long legs pressed against Holly's knee, and she found it difficult to think at all.

"Let's go into Tulsa to the Golden Pan," Sue said.

"Sounds good to me," Jeff added, pressing his knee against Holly's.

Holly moved her legs and pressed closer to the outside of the car, trying to give Jeff more room in the crowded leg space. "The Golden Pan is okay with me," she said.

When they pulled onto the Broken Arrow Expressway, the car seemed to take flight. Holly wanted to peer over Mike's shoulder to check the speedometer, but she knew she couldn't. Suddenly, all she could think of was getting to Tulsa safely and getting out of the car. The good part was that they would be there in ten minutes instead of the usual twenty, she thought. It was nice in a way. It didn't give any of them much time to begin a conversation in the car. And with Mike's loud music reverberating from the radio speakers behind Holly's head, she and Jeff could do little more than smile at each other.

"This place is packed tonight," Sue said as they pulled into the parking lot.

"Maybe we should have gone back over to Manney Mario's," Mike said. "They weren't too crowded last night."

"Last night wasn't Friday night, either," Sue said.

They all got out of the car and walked toward the door, and Holly wondered how Sue and Mike could have gone out last night. She knew about the lie Sue had told her parents last Saturday so she could go out with Mike. But what did she tell them last night? Or had they given Sue permission to single-date already?

Inside the Golden Pan, the lights were dimmed and wine-bottle candles dotted each booth and table. The aroma of hot, spicy pizza and crusty garlic bread hung heavily in the air and seemed to cling to each of them as they walked through the door.

"How about that booth over there in the corner," Sue said, pointing to the far side of the room.

"Didn't your mama ever tell you not to point?" Jeff teased.

"I can point if I want to," Sue said, threading her arm in Mike's. "Can't I, Mike?"

Mike took her hand and unwound her arm. "Sure," he said. "But why don't I just hold onto this little hand and we'll keep you out of trouble."

Everyone but Holly laughed at Mike's comment as they wove their way through the tables to the booth in the back corner.

"I want that sausage pizza with gobs of cheese," Sue said, sliding into the booth. "And some of that garlic bread, too, Mike. That stuff is so good with all the melted mozzarella cheese."

"What would you like, Holly?" Jeff asked.

"Sausage is fine with me." At least this way maybe Mike and Jeff can split the check in half and it wouldn't be so costly for either one of them, she thought.

When the waitress came by for the order, Mike said, "Small sausage, lots of cheese, garlic bread, and four large Cokes." As she turned to leave, he added, "We'd like the Cokes now, please."

Mike settled back in the booth and shifted closer to Sue. "It takes forever to get your order here, so I thought those Cokes in those big frosted mugs might taste pretty good while we're waiting."

A hush fell over the table as each of them sipped Coke from frosted mugs.

"Well, now, this is an exciting group," Sue said. "Give 'em a Coke and they take a nap."

"We're just catching our breath," Jeff said. "Besides, we all knew you'd be the first one to speak. We were just waiting."

Sue wiggled in her seat. "Let's talk about—" She rolled her blue eyes and pulled at a red curl and pretended to look thoughtful. "Let's talk about me." She giggled. "You know, I've been working every day after school with Marla. Been practicing cheers so I can try out for one of the basketball cheerleading squads."

"How's it going?" Jeff asked.

"Great. Marla says I'm doing really well for a beginner."

"If cheerleader is what you're after, I can't think of a better teacher than Marla," Jeff said. "She really knows her stuff."

Holly's gaze traveled from one person at the table to the other. As her eyes focused on each of them, her mind busily made brief notations.

Mike. Tall, broad shoulders, brown eyes. Sort of lumberjack-looking, Holly thought.

Mike was one of those guys who had the words "football player" written all over him. He reminded her of the pro ball players she watched on television occasionally with her dad.

Then there was Sue. She envied her friend's ability to be at ease no matter what the situation. Sue's curly red hair hugged her head tightly and her bright green eyes sparkled as she spoke. She looks different tonight somehow, Holly thought. Was it her unaccustomed makeup—the sea-green eye shadow on her eyelids and the tawny blush on her cheeks?

Holly glanced at Jeff out of the corner of her eye. He was tall and had broad shoulders. He seemed older than the others—more like a college guy or a man just entering a profession. It bothered her to feel as though she were sitting beside a man. She knew that talking to him this evening wouldn't be as easy as it had been at Marla's party with fifty other kids her age. And it definitely wasn't going to be as easy as leaning against the hood of Bob Anderson's old red car and talking to him about soccer.

When Holly drew herself back to the conversation, Mike was just finishing a dissertation on how well the Westview High Rebels were playing that year.

"I love going to the games and cheering

with the pep club," Sue said. "It's a lot of fun. Especially since we've been winning."

"You've picked a good time to get onto the cheerleading squad, too," Mike said. "This year's basketball team should be the best we've had in the three years I've been at Westview. A lot of the players from last year are coming back."

Jeff turned to Holly and looked at her as though he had just remembered that she was there.

"You're in the pep club, aren't you, Holly?" he asked.

"Sure. Don't you remember Marla telling you that I was, that night at the party?" Holly remembered talking about the pep club. Why didn't Jeff? What else didn't he remember about her? That party was only a little over a week ago.

"You know, you ought to try to get on the drill team next year," Jeff said. "Of course, it's too late to make the team this year, but next spring when they have the tryouts you ought to go for it."

"Maybe so," Holly said, feeling that at the moment she could think of nothing worse than being on the drill team. Besides, with any luck, she would be playing soccer with a classic team.

"Yeah. You girls are heading down the right

146

track, for sure," Mike said. "Everybody who is anybody is either a cheerleader or on the drill team. You know?"

"I know," Sue said. "Being a cheerleader has been my greatest goal since the day school opened."

"Well, when you're a cheerleader or on the drill team, you're just naturally with a different group of kids," Jeff said smugly. "Kind of like playing football." He took a gulp of his Coke. "Take me and Mike here. We don't have time to hang around with guys who aren't on the team. Everybody we know is on our side."

Holly listened to the conversation about football and cheerleading and felt herself sinking to the corner of the booth. *Now I know what my dad meant all those times he talked about going places and feeling like a fifth wheel,* she thought. *If they'd only talk about something I knew something about.*

Holly watched Mike try to balance a teaspoon on the tip of his finger. When Sue started laughing because he dropped it, Holly wished that she could be instantly transported back in time to her soccer practice that afternoon with Bob.

I could talk to him, she thought. *If we ran out of things to talk about, we always had soccer to fall back on.*

Soccer. That was something she liked to

talk about. It was something that Sue knew about, too. When the talk among Mike, Sue, and Jeff subsided, Holly seized the moment and spoke.

"Did any of you go to the Tulsa Roughers game last Saturday night?"

Her question was greeted by blank faces. "It was really exciting," she said. "They made the winning goal in the last minute of the game."

Sue sipped her Coke and didn't answer.

"I didn't go," Jeff said. "I'm not into soccer much anymore. Quit that when I was a kid."

"Oh, well—uh—my folks and I usually try to make all the pro soccer games," Holly said. "My parents like soccer. We'll probably go to the game tomorrow night too."

"Me and my folks are going over to Stillwater tomorrow to the Oklahoma State/Oklahoma University game," Mike said.

"Man, I'd give anything to see that game," Jeff said eagerly. "Oklahoma's messed up the last couple of games. The Pokes just might beat them."

"They might," Mike agreed. "That would sure be something to see."

Holly felt awkward. I can't talk to them about what they want to talk about, and they aren't interested in what I want to talk about, she thought. She ate slowly and was the last one to finish. But when they climbed into the sports car, they still had thirty minutes to spare.

"It's nine-thirty," Mike said from the driver's seat. "Want to go for a cruise toward the Muskogee Turnpike and back before we go home?"

Sue and Jeff both said yes. Holly's heart began to pound. The thought of going one hundred miles an hour in a car over which she had no control terrified her.

"I think you better take me home first," she said.

Though Mike had started the car, he turned around in his seat to look at Holly. Sue turned to stare at her, and so did Jeff.

"I—I'm beginning to get sick to my stomach. Must have been too much pizza," she lied. "I didn't say anything before we left the table, because I didn't want to ruin everybody's evening."

Mike nodded. "Sure, Holly. I'll take you right home. Gee, you should have said something."

"Well, it's been a gradual thing. It's pretty bad now, though."

"I wondered why you were being so quiet," Jeff said.

The ride home was quick and quiet with no one in the car speaking, not even Sue.

"I'll walk you to your door," Jeff said, as the car stopped in front of Holly's house.

When she reached the porch, Holly turned to Jeff. "I had a nice time, Jeff," she began. "Thanks a lot."

"I had a good time, too. . . ." Jeff said hurriedly as he bounded down the porch steps. "See you at school." His voice was muffled by the closing car door.

Holly could hear Sue's high giggle above the squealing of the tires as Mike drove away.

10

Holly waited impatiently in her mother's car for Bob to arrive.

"Did he say anything at the game yesterday about being late?" her mother asked.

"He wasn't at the game," Holly said. "And he's always early. He told me he makes it a point to arrive everywhere early."

"It's a shame that he didn't see your game," Judy said. "You all played almost as well as the Roughers did last night. You have a really good team this year," she said. "We're glad that this boy is helping you. It shows."

Holly could hardly concentrate on her mother's words for thinking about Bob. She thought about the way she had rushed away from practice Friday night because of her date with Jeff and what a terrible time she had had once she was with Jeff. I probably did something to make Bob mad, she told herself. He's probably cancelled the practices indefinitely and just didn't tell me.

"I think these practices are helping," Holly said, sensing that her mother was waiting for a response.

Holly ran her fingers through her hair and propped her elbow beside the car window. Suddenly, in the rear view mirror outside she saw an old, red car approaching. Her heart pounded in her throat and she turned to be sure it was really him.

"He's here!" Holly said. As soon as the words were out, she wished she had sounded more casual.

She opened her car door, then looked back inside at her mother. "Give us about an hour, Mom," she said, smiling. "Maybe a few minutes more."

Bob stepped out of his car. "Sorry I'm late." He started gathering his equipment from the back seat. "Had a little car trouble. She decided she didn't want to start." He turned to Holly and threw a soccer ball to her. "But I got her working again."

"Guess a guy just has to learn how to treat a lady to get her to do what he wants," Holly teased.

"Right." Bob smiled. He placed the soccer ball he was carrying on the ground. "Time to get serious," he said. "Are you ready?"

"Ready," Holly said, watching the autumn wind play with his sandy blond hair.

At the end of the practice, Holly helped Bob load the equipment into his car.

"Is your mom coming for you today?" Bob asked, throwing the last soccer ball into the back seat.

"Yes. I'm sure she'll be here in a few minutes," Holly said, taking her position against the hood of his car and waiting for him to join her.

"You know, it's such a gorgeous day," Bob said, walking around to the hood of his car. "Would you like to run over to the Orbit for a Coke?"

Holly's pulse quickened. "I need to check with my parents first, if that's okay."

"Sure," Bob said. "No problem. I thought since we were through a few minutes early, I'd run you by your house to check. How would that be?"

"That would be super."

When Holly and Bob drove into Miller Park, Holly felt like pinching herself to be sure she was really there. The Coke at the Orbit had been fun. But when Bob asked her if she wanted to go for a drive through Miller Park, that was almost too much for Holly's sense of reality to bear.

"You want to get out?" Bob asked, as they approached a beautifully landscaped parking area.

"Sure."

Bob parked, walked around to Holly's side of the car, and opened the door for her. She followed him along the slope that extended from the parking area to a grassy knoll dotted with park benches. She took a seat at one end of a narrow bench, and Bob seated himself at the other end.

He reached down and picked a three-leaf clover from the clover patch that ran under the bench.

"You're getting good," he said, twirling the clover in his fingers. "Really good."

"Do you mean my lessons are paying off?" she smiled.

"I don't think you can call them lessons," Bob said. "I just show you what I know and you go with it. You're really something. I mean it," he said. "You aren't going to need much more coaching from me. I've taught you almost all I know."

"That's a lot," Holly said. She didn't want to hear him talk about her lessons coming to an end. She watched him hold the clover in the air and let the breeze take it from his fingers. I'm just beginning to know him, she thought.

I've just discovered that I like him. Really like him for who he is and not only for the way he looks. She sighed inwardly. I wish I knew if he liked me. "You know, you're good enough that you could probably become a pro someday," she said aloud. "Have you ever thought about that?"

"Only all the time. When I graduate, I'm going to go to college over at Carson. They've got a good soccer program there. It's part of their athletics program."

"Abby told me your mom was a soccer advisor at Midwestern. That they were trying to get a girl's soccer program started there. Don't they have a good men's soccer program?"

"Sure. Their program is probably as good as Carson's." Bob plucked another sprig of clover from the patch beneath their bench. "I guess I want to go to Carson so I'll know I made the team on my own." He threw the clover sprig to the ground, then clasped his hands. "For some weird reason, it's important for me to know that I've made it on my own. If I went to Midwestern and made their team, I'd always wonder if I made it on my own abilities or if I was placed on the team because my mom was one of their advisors."

Holly smiled. "I see what you mean. I've never really thought about doing things to prove that I can."

"You might not think about it, but you do it all the time."

"What do you mean?"

"Your soccer," Bob said. "You're the only one who can control how you play."

"Yeah. But when I'm bad I'm the one who gets the credit for that too."

Bob chuckled. "I guess it's all just part of the deal. But you see what I mean, don't you?"

Holly nodded. "I see."

She watched white, billowy clouds glide across the sky and felt the cool autumn breeze whisper across her face.

"When Abby told me that Midwestern was thinking about starting a girl's soccer team—" She hesitated for a moment, almost afraid to go on. "—well, I thought I might go there when I graduate from high school. I even had the crazy thought that I might try for a soccer scholarship." She blurted out the words, hoping Bob wouldn't think her plan was ridiculous. Before he could speak, she said, "You know, if you're not a straight A student and your parents aren't loaded, you've gotta be thinking all the time about how you're going to get into or through college."

Bob smiled at her. "I think you've got a great plan." Then he winked and said, "And I've got a feeling you'll make it."

"I hope so," Holly said, as casually as she could. "My dad would love it."

She watched the breeze play with Bob's blond hair, and her gaze traced the faint lines of a smile that still lingered on his lips. Never before, she thought as his gaze met hers, I've never felt this way before.

Bob stopped the car at the curb in front of Holly's house rather than pulling into her driveway. "Whoa, girl," he said, patting the steering wheel.

Holly ran her fingers over the cloth-covered bench seat. "I've got to admit that I'm sort of beginning to understand your feelings about this car." She tapped the seat.

Bob placed his hand on Holly's before she could pull it from the space on the seat between them.

"You'll like her better the more you're around her," he said. He glanced down at his hand over Holly's and then back at her face. "Hey, I really did have a great time," he said. "I'm glad you could go to the Orbit with me this afternoon."

"Me, too. I had a great time, too," Holly said, barely able to force the words out above a whisper.

She felt her hand tremble as he leaned toward her. Closer and closer he came until his lips met hers. Holly closed her eyes and felt every muscle in her body dissolve at the touch of his warm mouth upon hers. When he pulled away and she opened her eyes once again, she could hardly breathe.

He didn't say a word, just gently squeezed her hand and then got out of the car and came around to open Holly's door.

Though his kiss had lasted only an instant, it left her trembling. Bob took her hand and helped her out of the car. He walked her to her front porch, then said, "I'll see you next Friday at practice."

Holly's heart took a dive. Friday was five days away. "Sure. See you then," she said, as cheerfully as she could. "Thanks again for inviting me this afternoon."

She turned to walk into her house and heard his footsteps on the driveway as he walked to his car. She went into her bedroom and closed the door. Their kiss had meant nothing to him. She was still just the girl that he coached.

Holly walked through the front door of Westview High and made her way through the crowded halls to her locker. She glanced at the faces she passed, wondering if she'd see Sue in their midst. Funny, she thought, opening her locker. I didn't see or talk to Sue all weekend, and I didn't really miss her.

Holly exchanged the set of books in her arms for the ones lying on the bottom of her locker.

"Hey, Holly," a deep voice called from behind her.

From her squatting position in front of the locker, she noticed the cowboy boots and jeans first, as the pair of feet stopped beside her. She glanced up and saw Jeff standing beside her.

"Jeff? What are you doing here?"

"Oh, I was in the neighborhood and just thought I'd drop by," Jeff said. "How are you feeling?"

"I'm feeling fine," Holly said. "Why?"

Jeff gave her a curious look. "I was just wondering. You said you were really getting sick the other night, and I just wondered if you were feeling better now."

"I—I was sick," she said. "I was really sick Friday night. But I was better by Saturday."

"That's good," Jeff said. "I was hoping it wasn't anything serious." He started to walk away, but then he turned to her again. "Say, Holly. I was wondering if you might want to go out for hamburgers after the game Friday night."

Holly thought about Friday being her practice session with Bob. But then she thought about having to go to the game and sit with the pep club again. Since she would be at the game anyway, she might as well go for hamburgers with Jeff.

She gazed into Jeff's laughing blue eyes and

felt as though things might be different this time if she went out with him. Bob isn't going to call me, she told herself. He said he'd see me at practice Friday night.

"I'd like to go for hamburgers," Holly said. "Want to ask Sue and Mike to come along, too?" she asked, feeling certain that her parents would approve as long as Sue was along.

Jeff winked at her. "I'll ask them," he said, smiling. "I'll give you a call later and let you know."

Holly closed her locker and started for her first-hour class. A few steps ahead of her she saw a familiar-looking blonde.

"Abby?" Holly called.

Abby turned and smiled. "How are the old soccer practices coming along?" A mischievous grin tugged at the corners of her mouth and her blue eyes. "You did have soccer practice yesterday, didn't you?"

"I had practice yesterday," Holly said. "And that's not all I had," she added, unable to resist the temptation to make Abby think there was really something between her and Bob.

Abby giggled. "Well, don't stop now," she said. "Tell me more. Tell me more."

Holly tried to act nonchalant. "Oh, it wasn't much really," she said, hoping that her manner would make Abby even more curious. "Bob just took me out for a Coke afterward."

She paused for a second, then said, "In his car. And then we went to Miller Park."

Abby's eyes widened. "To Miller Park! Holly, you mean he really took you to Miller Park? That's great! What happened then?"

The memory of his kiss hung in Holly's mind, and a shiver darted through her as she recalled exactly how it felt. It was so special, she told herself. Too special to tell about.

"Well?" Abby pressed. "What else happened?"

"We just sat on a bench and talked," Holly said. "And then he took me home. That's all." Holly couldn't tell her about the kiss. It was too important to share with anyone.

"Sounds to me as though he likes you," Abby said. "Do you like him? I mean really like him?"

Holly wanted to shout, "Of course I really like him," but what was the point? Why should she admit, even to Abby, that she was in love with a boy who only thought of improving her soccer?

She shrugged her shoulders and raised her eyebrows mysteriously.

As they turned the corner and approached their first-hour classroom, Holly saw Sue.

"Holly!" Sue shouted, rushing up to them. "I've been looking all over the building for you."

"Why? What's wrong?"

"There's nothing wrong," Sue said. "I just wanted to talk to you about our date with Jeff and Mike the other night."

A sick feeling settled in the bottom of Holly's stomach. She didn't mind talking to Sue about their date. But she didn't want to talk to her about it in front of Abby. What must she think? Holly wondered, glancing at Abby out of the corner of her eye. I've just told her I was with Bob yesterday, and Sue's just told her I was out with Jeff.

"Holly, I think I'm going to go on to class. I've got a few things I need to do before class starts."

"Okay," Holly said. She forced a smile and said, "I'll be there in a couple of minutes."

Holly knew that Abby didn't have anything to do in class ahead of time. It was just her way of saying, "I can see I'm in the way here."

"Didn't you just have the best time with Jeff?" Sue said excitedly. "Didn't you think Mike had the neatest car you've ever seen?"

Holly's heart pounded harder and harder, and an "I've got to get out of here" feeling swept over her. She knew she should stay and talk to Sue, since they hadn't talked all weekend. But for some reason, she couldn't make herself do it.

"I had a good time," Holly said curtly.

She tried to step away from Sue, but Sue followed her every move.

"I saw Jeff this morning," Holly said. "He's invited me for hamburgers after the game Friday." She took a few more steps toward her classroom. "He's going to ask you and Mike, too."

"He is?" Sue asked. "That will be terrific."

11

We are the Rebels. The mighty, mighty Rebels," Holly screamed.

The cool night air wrapped itself around Holly and sent chills through her. I wish I'd worn my coat instead of this jacket, she thought.

When the cheer ended, all the girls in the pep club section of the stands screamed and yelled. All but Holly. She sat with her jacket pulled around her, unhappily wondering why Bob had cancelled their practice for the evening. She'd spent the whole week looking forward to their Friday practice. It had been five days since their Coke date and ride through Miller Park. Now all that she had to look forward to was her date with Jeff after the game and the hope of a practice session with Bob on Sunday afternoon.

Holly watched Marla and the other cheerleaders do jumps and spins and lead cheers on the ground at the foot of the stands. He said something came up, Holly thought, remembering clearly the telephone conversation with Bob a few hours earlier. Nothing more. No further explanation. Just, "Something's come up, and I won't be able to make it this afternoon. I'll talk to you Sunday about a make-up time."

Holly applauded as the cheerleaders completed another cheer. I guess it was good that we didn't practice, she told herself. At least I got to spend a little time on myself before Sue picked me up for the game.

The noise from the girls on the bleachers around her mingled with shouting voices across the stadium. She glanced around her. There must have been forty or fifty girls, all wearing the same kind of Westview High pep club T-shirts as Holly wore. For someone who was going to be a leader and step away from the crowd at the beginning of school, I haven't done very well, Holly thought.

She thought about the plan she and Sue had had. We were going to be leaders and get in with the popular crowd. Sue's getting in with them, I suppose, Holly told herself. And I am a leader of sorts. I'm team captain for the Stingers. I guess the girls on the team look up to me for help and instructions for the games.

Holly's thoughts drifted away from the football field. In her mind's eye she could see her team playing and Bob Anderson standing on the sidelines. Bob said he has to do things on his own to feel good about it, Holly thought.

Sue jumped into the air and inadvertently jostled Holly. "A touchdown," Sue shrieked. "Did you see it? Mike made a touchdown."

"Sure, sure, I saw it," Holly said. "It was great." She pulled herself back to the real world of Westview High. Face it, Holly Malone, she said to herself. You're in high school and football is the game. Soccer just isn't in with these kids.

She watched Marla wave her arms and shake the blue-and-gold pompoms in the air. They are the leaders, Holly thought.

She thought about Sue and her pursuit of basketball cheerleader status. Sue probably had the right idea. The cheerleaders were the only leaders, really. But Holly knew that she couldn't drop soccer to devote her time to cheerleading now, even if she wanted to. She had sold her parents on the idea of private coaching and they were all hoping that Holly's soccer would eventually lead to an athletic scholarship to college. No, dropping soccer was out of the question.

Half-time was closing in on them and Sue seemed to be yelling louder and with more enthusiasm with each passing second on the clock.

Holly pulled her jacket tighter and glanced at Marla's bare legs, almost blue from the chilly night breeze. I don't think I'd want to be a cheerleader even if I could, Holly thought. She thought of how the cool air stung her legs on the soccer field and of how she didn't even notice the temperature once the game began. She watched Marla do a flip. When you're a cheerleader, you share the win the football team has made, Holly thought. But when you're on the soccer field, the win is yours.

The trip from the stadium to the hamburger stand was probably made in record time.

Sue quickly seated herself in the round corner booth.

"Hurry. Sit here before all the other kids get here," Sue said.

She sat in the center of the half-moon-shaped booth and Holly sat beside her. Mike and Jeff took their places at the ends.

"This is pretty cozy," Sue said, snuggling up beside Mike. She kissed Mike on the cheek and threaded her arm through his.

Holly felt Jeff move in closer to her. She took a sip of ice water and pretended that she didn't feel Jeff against her. Then she cleared her throat and said, "Well, it was a great game, wasn't it?" She tugged at Sue's arm. "Didn't you think it was a great game, Sue?"

"A great game," she agreed.

Jeff nudged closer to Holly again. She felt him breathing at her neck, and she froze. His warm lips brushed softly across her cheek and ear, sending an electrical shock wave rippling through her body.

"Jeff," she said. "Stop it."

"What's the matter? You can do it in the park, but you can't do it in a restaurant?"

"I don't know what you mean," Holly said, feeling the full stare of Sue's and Mike's eyes at her back.

"Oh, come on, Holly," Jeff said. "I saw you in Miller Park Sunday afternoon with that guy. Everybody knows why kids go to Miller Park."

"Yeah. To make out," Sue said.

"Make out? I wasn't making out in Miller Park. I was just talking."

"Talking. Making out. What difference does it make? You were out with me on Friday and then with this other guy on Sunday. Marla never told me you got around so," Jeff said.

Holly's face grew hot. "Bob is a friend," she said. "Besides, you don't own me, Jeff. We're not even going together, so I don't see what's the big deal."

"She's right, you know," Mike mocked. "You're not going with her, Jeff."

Holly clenched her fists under the table.

Jeff looked at her and shrugged. "Guess Mike's right. It's a free country."

"Everybody's got to be somewhere," Sue chirped.

Holly glared at all of them and waited in silence for Jeff to offer more of an apology than "It's a free country." When nothing more was said, she made herself smile. She raised her Coke into the air. "Since everybody's got to be somewhere, and we're all here together, let's do what we came here for." She moved the cup in Mike's direction. "To Mike. In honor of his touchdown tonight."

Holly was eager to get to the playing field the next morning for the soccer game. She stepped out of the car and was at the sideline before her parents could get out and lock the car doors.

Where's Abby? she wondered, scanning the field for black-and-gold uniforms. Abby will know what happened to Bob last night, why he canceled our lesson. How could she help knowing? She lives two doors away.

Holly wished now that she hadn't spent most of the night awake. Her eyes burned in the light of the early morning sun, and her shoulders ached the way they sometimes did when she sat at her desk too long studying.

"Who are you looking for?" Abby said, coming up behind Holly.

Holly jumped. "You scared the daylights out of me," she said. "I was looking for you."

"You found me. What'cha need?"

"Information," Holly said. "I want to know if you know what happened to Bob last night. He cancelled our practice."

"Cancelled your practice?" Abby asked. "Didn't he call you or anything?"

"Oh, Abby, of course he called me. He called and said that something had come up and that he'd try to set a make-up time with me on Sunday." Holly glanced at the ground. "I just wondered if you might have seen him or something."

Abby sighed. "I'm sorry, Holly. I don't have any idea what happened to him. My folks and I were gone all evening, and when we got home, I really didn't notice if Bob's car was at his house or not."

"Oh," Holly said softly. She shrugged her shoulders and tried to smile. "Don't think anything about it," she said as lightly as she could. "It's nothing. He said something came up, and I just thought you might have known what. No big deal."

The phone was ringing when Holly and her parents stepped through the door.

"I'll get it," Holly yelled, running through the kitchen into the living room. "Hello."

"Hello, Holly? This is Jeff," the voice on the other end said.

Holly's first impulse was to hang up and walk away as though no one had called.

"Listen. I've called to tell you that I know you didn't have a very good time last night," Jeff said before Holly could speak. "And I'm sorry. Really. I'd like to take you out for a Coke, though. Maybe things would be different with just the two of us."

"I can't go," Holly said.

"I see. Really. I do," Jeff said. "And I don't blame you a bit for being sore." He cleared his throat. "I've got Dad's car for a while, and I'd feel a lot better if you'd let me buy you a Coke, though, and try to make it up to you." Jeff paused for a moment. "How about it, Holly? What do you say?"

"I'll ask my folks," she said reluctantly. "Just a minute."

Jeff stopped the car at the curb. He slid his arm across the back of Holly's seat. "Would you go to the game with me on Thursday night?"

"The game?"

"Yeah. You do remember there is a game this Thursday night, don't you? Aren't you cheering for it?"

"Yes, I guess I am," Holly said.

Jeff's blue eyes smoldered as he waited for Holly's answer.

Their date hadn't been too bad, she reasoned. Besides, she certainly didn't have any other boys knocking down her door to ask her out.

"Sure, thanks for asking me," she said.

The words had just left her lips when Jeff leaned toward her and claimed her lips as his. The warmth of his kiss surged through her, and Holly pushed him away.

"I've got to go in," she said breathlessly. Her head was spinning.

Jeff started to get out of the car, but Holly stopped him.

"No. You don't need to walk me to the door," she said, trying to compose herself. "I'll see you in school."

"Okay," Jeff said. "See you then."

Holly walked through the front door and toward her bedroom.

"Holly? Is that you?" her mother called.

"Yes, Mom. I was just going into the bedroom to study for a while before dinner."

"Bob called while you were out," Judy Malone said.

Holly's pulse quickened. "Did he say what time he wants to get together for practice tomorrow?"

"That's why he called," Mrs. Malone said. "He said he wouldn't be able to make it for your session tomorrow afternoon."

12

Holly didn't know how long she had been lying across her bed. Maybe an hour. Possibly two. It had been some time since church and Sunday dinner. It didn't matter really. She had gone there to think, but even now she hadn't resolved anything.

She heard someone gently ease open her bedroom door behind her and turned to see her mother peeking in at her.

"I'm sorry, sweetheart. I didn't mean to disturb you. I thought you might have gone to sleep."

"I'm not asleep, Mom. Just resting before I start my homework."

A worry line creased her mother's brow as

she pushed the door open a little farther. "You're not getting sick, are you?"

Holly tried to smile. "No, I'm not getting sick, Mom."

Mrs. Malone entered her daughter's bedroom and closed the door behind her. She took a seat on the edge of Holly's bed. "Mind telling me what's upsetting you?" she asked, placing her outstretched hand at the center of Holly's back. "Or is that something that I shouldn't know?"

Holly sighed and felt the tears welling up inside her. At any given moment they might begin streaming down her cheeks.

Her mother moved her hand slowly across the small of Holly's back, and it reminded Holly of her childhood when her mother would rub her back or massage her fingertips across Holly's forehead.

"I would tell you, Mom," Holly said, "if I knew what I wanted to tell." She rolled over onto her back and slipped her arms under her head. "I'm just confused."

Her mother smiled at Holly. "I've been confused a lot of times, but one way or another, I usually found the solution. Want to see if one of my solutions fits your problem?"

"I'll try," Holly sighed. She took another deep breath and let it out slowly. "I thought high school was supposed to be a time for having fun."

Her mother nodded. "It is. Part of it, anyway."

Holly rubbed her forehead and wished she could press all the thoughts from her mind. "See, when Sue and I started school this year, we decided right from the beginning that we were going to move away from all the average kids we've gone to school with. We were going to become leaders. You know—a couple of the biggies in the school."

Holly smiled wryly. "Sue has moved away all right. We're barely friends now." She frowned and tried to make some sense of it all. "Sue's going to try out for cheerleader when basketball season gets here. And I'm a nothing in the pep club. A real nobody, as Sue would say. I don't even like the pep club. The only reason I joined it in the first place was because Sue wanted me to. She said it would help us get in with the popular crowd." Holly rolled over on her stomach once again. "I guess it worked for her."

Mrs. Malone placed her hand on Holly's back once again. "It might have worked for Sue," she said. "But don't you think it's nice that what works for one person doesn't necessarily have to work for another? Aren't you glad that we aren't all alike?" She smiled. "Maybe Sue and her new friends truly love cheerleading and football as much as you love your soccer. That's the joy of all of us being different. We can choose and do the things we like to do and leave what we don't like to those people who do like them."

Sort of makes sense, Holly thought.

Judy Malone stood up to leave. "Do things because you want to do them, Holly. Not because someone else is doing them, or because someone else wants you to."

Holly watched her mother walk toward the door.

"Mom," Holly said, "why do guys think so much about their cars and act as though nothing else is important?"

Her mother grinned. "I think if the truth be known, men's first loves are their cars, and their women come second."

Holly got to the field just as Coach Gordon blew his whistle to begin. She looked for Abby but didn't see her. Her gaze traveled across the field and the parking lot. She tried to tell herself that she wasn't looking for Bob.

Holly noticed a short, thin woman with Coach Gordon and wondered who she was and what she was doing there. She really thought it was strange when Coach had them go through a few of their drills individually. After Holly finished her workout, she saw the woman making notes on a tablet.

On the way home, Holly thought about Bob. Why doesn't he want to work with me anymore? she wondered. What have I done? And why didn't Abby show up for practice?

Holly walked through the back door and into the kitchen. She started to make herself a sandwich, then decided to change her clothes first.

"Jeff called," Hugh Malone said, as Holly walked through the living room. "Said he'd be by to pick you up at seven tomorrow to go to the game."

The sudden reminder of her date with Jeff caught Holly off guard. She answered, "Okay," and then walked on into her room.

She stripped off her clothes and slipped on her robe. She picked up her hairbrush and began brushing the short strands of brown hair away from her face. Then she stared at her reflection in the dresser mirror and placed the brush on the dresser top again.

"I can't stand it," she said to her reflection. "I just can't stand this anymore."

Holly left her bedroom and went into the living room. She glanced around the room and, seeing that both of her parents were in another part of the house, she picked up the phone and dialed Jeff's number.

She took a deep breath to steady herself, then let it out slowly as she heard Jeff's voice in her ear.

"Hi. This is Holly," she said, her voice cracking a bit.

"Hi, Holly. Did your dad tell you that I called?"

Holly's stomach drew into a ball. "He told me," she said. "That's why I'm calling, Jeff. I can't make it."

Jeff was silent for a moment and then said, "I'm sorry, Holly. Do you want to make it some other time then?"

"No. No. I don't." Holly felt herself tremble and she knew she was going to have to hurry and end the conversation before she backed out.

"I don't want to go out with you anymore, Jeff." She quickly added, "It's not you. You're really a nice guy. It's just that we're so different. We just don't like the same things."

She waited for a few seconds for him to say something, and when he didn't, she said, "I'm dropping out of the pep club, too, and I won't be going to the games anymore. That just doesn't seem to be my thing." She hung up quickly before he could remonstrate or respond.

It was all Holly could do to go to school the next day. She carefully avoided going anywhere that she thought she might run into Sue or Jeff. But there was no escaping Sue during fifth hour, and Sue wasn't about to let her get away.

"I saw Jeff at noon, and he told me what you did last night," Sue said as they were leaving the classroom. "Are you crazy?"

Holly knew Sue wouldn't understand, and she wondered if she should even try to explain. "I had to do it," Holly said simply. "I'm trying to be my own person. It's something I've got to do. For me."

"I think you've flipped. You better reconsider."

"Can't," Holly said. "I've already dropped out of the pep club, and I still feel that I've made the right decision about Jeff. We're just too different."

"You haven't even given yourself a chance to find out," Sue said. "People can change. Look at me." Sue threw her arm into the air, then slapped her side. "When school started, I was into soccer and not really much of anything else. But I knew there was other stuff I wanted to be into. Heck, next semester I'm going to make it on the cheerleading squad. I'm excited about the new things I'm into."

"I know you are," Holly said. "And I tried to be excited about the pep club and that stuff too. But, it didn't work. Don't you see? My dropping out of the pep club is no different than when you dropped out of soccer at the start of the season. It's crazy. But my mom and I were talking about this very thing just the other night. She said that high school is a time for having fun, but it's also a time for learning who we are. Maybe we're just growing up, Sue, and finding out what kind of interests these two different people have."

"Maybe so," Sue said hesitantly. She stared at Holly, opened her mouth, then closed it and stared again. "I've got to get to class," she said finally. Before Holly could answer, Sue turned and walked down the hall away from her.

Holly had a quiet dinner at home with her parents that night. She spent most of her time at the table wondering if she was happy or sad about not having to go to the football game and cheer that evening. She picked at her food, and when she could eat no more, she asked to be excused and went to her bedroom, her retreat from the world and all its confusing problems.

She hadn't been in her room very long when she heard a light knock on the door.

Her mother pushed open the door and smiled. "Get up and make yourself beautiful, kid," she teased. "You've got company. Bob's here."

Holly whirled out of her bedroom and

passed her mother in the hallway on her way to the living room. She slowed as she approached the foyer and saw Bob standing in the room talking with her father.

"Hi, Bob," Holly said. Her heart beat so loudly that she was afraid everyone in the room would notice.

"Hi," Bob said. He glanced down at the carpet and then back at Holly. "I hope I didn't interrupt anything. It just dawned on me on my way over here that I should have called first."

Holly knew she was grinning from ear to ear, but she couldn't stop herself. "That's okay," she said. "I wasn't doing much."

She glanced at the clock on the wall behind her father and saw that it was almost eight o'clock. Kick-off time. Holly bit her lip. I've never been so happy to miss a football game in all my life, Holly thought. Never.

Bob slid his hands into the pockets of his cream-colored jacket. "If you're not busy, I wondered if you might like to go for a Coke with me," he said. He shrugged. "I probably owe you more than that for not showing up at practice the last couple of times."

Holly wondered if he was ever going to tell her why he had cancelled those two sessions. She had promised herself that she would never ask.

She glanced at her mother and saw her give an approving nod, as did her father.

"I'd love to," Holly told him.

"Great," Bob said. He walked with her to the front door and helped her with her jacket. "You know, the reason I didn't call before I came over was because I was out trying the new engine I put in my car. It's a killer. I've spent the last two weeks working on it. Day and night. But she's really something now. I can't wait for you to ride in it."

Holly laughed. "Why should we wait?" she asked. "Let's go!"

"She's almost like a new girl now," Bob said, smiling.

As they walked down the drive, Bob said, "I'm sorry that our practices got so messed up."

"Oh, that's all right," Holly said.

"No, it isn't all right." Bob opened the car door and tucked her inside. When he was in the car too, he turned to her and said, "I told you before that I don't operate that way. I like to be places early, and I make it a point to hold to my commitments."

He started the car. "Purrs like a little kitten," he said proudly. "It took nearly two weeks, and it delayed two of your practices, I'm sorry to say, but I finally got that engine in. A babe, huh?"

Holly giggled. "Sure is," she said.

As they pulled away from the curb, Bob said, "You didn't have plans for this evening, did you?"

"No." Holly pushed her hair behind one ear and said, "I was planning to go to the Westview High football game, but I changed my mind."

"I don't like football too much," Bob said.

"You don't like football?" Holly asked, her eyes widening. "I thought everybody in the world except me liked football."

Holly saw him grin and shake his head as he steered them in the direction of the Orbit. They pulled in and Bob ordered two Cokes through the order phone.

"Are we going to get together at the usual time tomorrow for practice, now that you've got your car running again?" she asked.

Bob took a sip of Coke and shook his head. "No. I talked to Coach Gordon before I came to your house. We both agree that you don't really need those practice sessions any longer."

"Guess that means we won't be seeing too much of each other from now on, then." She tried to keep her tone casual, even though her heart was sinking.

"Oh, I don't know about that," Bob said. He shifted in the car seat and turned to face her.

"You know that lady who watched your practice yesterday?"

Holly cocked an eyebrow. "How do you know that there was a lady watching our practice? Were you there?"

"No, I wasn't there. That woman was my mom."

"Your mother? But what was she doing at our practice?"

Bob sighed and slumped in the seat. "I knew I couldn't see you tonight without telling you." He lifted his hand in the air between them. "But if I tell you, you have to promise that you won't tell that you know."

"I promise, I promise. What is it?"

"Mom was checking out some of the players on your team. The ones who received high marks yesterday won't have to try out for her classic team next season. She'll just notify them that they have been selected to join if they want to." He winked at Holly. "You're going to be asked to join. That's why Coach Gordon said we didn't need to practice any more."

"I can't believe it," Holly shouted. She grabbed Bob's hand and squeezed it tightly. "I just can't believe it!"

"I kind of thought you'd be surprised," he said. He looked at her as sternly as he could and said, "Remember, you can't tell."

"I won't tell," Holly said. She giggled. "I don't know how I'll keep from it. But I won't tell."

Bob started talking again. "You know, since we won't be seeing each other on the soccer field anymore, I think we ought to think about getting together once in a while."

Holly smiled and sipped her Coke.

"Well, now that I've got my car fixed up, and we don't have any more practice sessions, I'll probably have a lot more free time on my hands," Bob said.

"Maybe we sort of need a new beginning?" Holly said, grinning at Bob.

"Yeah. Yeah. That's a good idea," Bob answered. "A new beginning is exactly what we need." Bob placed his cup on the tray mounted outside the window on his side of the car and turned to Holly. "Did I ever tell you how I feel about your eyes?"

Holly laughed and said, "No."

"Well," Bob said. "I guess I didn't because I was too preoccupied with your feet."

Holly turned toward him in the seat and leaned her elbow on the seat back. "I'm glad your interest has moved from my feet to my eyes. 'You got great feet, kid,' doesn't really send me."

Bob laughed with her and gently slipped his hand over hers. He gazed into Holly's eyes, and slowly drew her closer to him. Without a word, he took her face in his hand and gently kissed her lips.

"Ready for a new beginning?" he whispered.

"Ready!" she answered above her pounding heart.

Four exciting First Love from Silhouette romances yours for 15 days—_free!_

If you enjoyed this First Love from Silhouette,® you'll want to read more! These are true-to-life romances about the things that matter most to you now—your friendships, dating, getting along in school, and learning about yourself. The stories could really happen, and the characters are so real they'll seem like friends.

Now you can get 4 First Love from Silhouette romances to look over for 15 days—absolutely free! If you decide not to keep them, simply return them and pay nothing. But if you enjoy them as much as we believe you will, keep them and pay the invoice enclosed with your trial shipment. You'll then become a member of the First Love from Silhouette℠ Book Club and will receive 4 more new First Love from Silhouette romances every month. You'll always be among the first to get them, and you'll never miss a new title. There is no minimum number of books to buy and you can cancel at any time. To receive your 4 books, mail the coupon below today.

First Love from Silhouette® is a service mark and a registered trademark of Simon & Schuster.

This offer expires May 31, 1984

First Love from Silhouette Book Club, Dept. FL-018
120 Brighton Road, P.O. Box 5020, Clifton, NJ 07015

Please send me 4 First Love from Silhouette romances to keep for 15 days, absolutely _free_. I understand I am not obligated to join the First Love from Silhouette Book Club unless I decide to keep them.

NAME_____
(Please print)

ADDRESS_____

CITY_____ STATE_____ ZIP_____

Signature_____
(If under 18, parent or guardian must sign)

First Love from Silhouette

THERE'S NOTHING QUITE AS SPECIAL AS A <u>FIRST LOVE.</u>

——— $1.75 each ———

2 ☐ GIRL IN THE ROUGH
Wunsch

3 ☐ PLEASE LET ME IN
Beckman

4 ☐ SERENADE
Marceau

6 ☐ KATE HERSELF
Erskine

7 ☐ SONGBIRD
Enfield

14 ☐ PROMISED KISS
Ladd

15 ☐ SUMMER ROMANCE
Diamond

16 ☐ SOMEONE TO LOVE
Bryan

17 ☐ GOLDEN GIRL
Erskine

18 ☐ WE BELONG TOGETHER
Harper

19 ☐ TOMORROW'S WISH
Ryan

20 ☐ SAY PLEASE!
Francis

——— $1.95 each ———

24 ☐ DREAM LOVER
Treadwell

26 ☐ A TIME FOR US
Ryan

27 ☐ A SECRET PLACE
Francis

29 ☐ FOR THE LOVE OF LORI
Ladd

30 ☐ A BOY TO DREAM ABOUT
Quinn

31 ☐ THE FIRST ACT
London

32 ☐ DARE TO LOVE
Bush

33 ☐ YOU AND ME
Johnson

34 ☐ THE PERFECT FIGURE
March

35 ☐ PEOPLE LIKE US
Haynes

36 ☐ ONE ON ONE
Ketter

37 ☐ LOVE NOTE
Howell

38 ☐ ALL-AMERICAN GIRL
Payton

39 ☐ BE MY VALENTINE
Harper

40 ☐ MY LUCKY STAR
Cassiday

41 ☐ JUST FRIENDS
Francis

42 ☐ PROMISES TO COME
Dellin

43 ☐ A KNIGHT TO REMEMBER
Martin

44 ☐ SOMEONE LIKE
JEREMY VAUGHN
Alexander

First Love from Silhouette

Lift Your Spirit This October With
THE MYSTERY KISS
by Elaine Harper

- -

FIRST LOVE, Department FL/4
1230 Avenue of the Americas
New York, NY 10020

Please send me the books I have checked above. I am enclosing $_____ (please add 50¢ to cover postage and handling. NYS and NYC residents please add appropriate sales tax). Send check or money order—no cash or C.O.D.'s please. Allow six weeks for delivery.

NAME _____

ADDRESS _____

CITY_____ STATE/ZIP_____

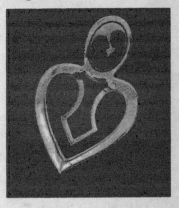

Silhouette ❤️ *Romance*

15-Day Free Trial Offer
6 Silhouette Romances

6 Silhouette Romances, free for 15 days! We'll send you 6 new Silhouette Romances to keep for 15 days, absolutely free! If you decide not to keep them, send them back to us. You pay nothing.

Free Home Delivery. But if you enjoy them as much as we think you will, keep them by paying the invoice enclosed with your free trial shipment. We'll pay all shipping and handling charges. You get the convenience of Home Delivery and we pay the postage and handling charge each month.

Don't miss a copy. The Silhouette Book Club is the way to make sure you'll be able to receive every new romance we publish before they're sold out. There is no minimum number of books to buy and you can cancel at any time.